Gone to the Rapture

(The Time Bubble Book 14)

By Jason Ayres

Cover art by:

Daniela Owergoor

http://dani-owergoor.deviantart.com/

Contents

Chapter One
July 2023

As the sun beat down on a glorious July afternoon, veteran lorry driver Jake Rogers was driving his HGV south on the M40. He was looking forward to getting back to his family in Oxford after a long journey down from Manchester.

Most of July had been wet and cool, a disappointment after a series of good summers. But today had brought a welcome change. The sky was a deep shade of blue, with fluffy white clouds scattered across the horizon. Fields of golden wheat and lush green pastures stretched out on either side of the motorway, dotted with patches of wildflowers and hedgerows. The trees along the roadside cast short shadows from a sun that was still high in the sky, their leaves rustling gently in the warm breeze.

As Jake drove past the junction nine exit for Bicester and on towards Oxford, he thought about his wife and teenage children and how much he was going to enjoy the evening ahead. It was his birthday, not a big one, that would be next year, but even so, he knew his wife would have gone all out for his special day. She always did. They had a barbecue planned and he couldn't wait to sink his teeth into her homemade burgers, not to mention the many other goodies she would have picked up from their favourite butcher in Oxford's famous Covered Market.

It was a home he was destined never to reach. He had not a hint of a warning of what was about to happen, or why, but if anyone had been peering into his cab at the fateful moment they would have seen something inexplicable; one second he was there, and the next he wasn't. He had simply disappeared from existence.

Without any pressure on the accelerator, the lorry began to slow down, but unfortunately, there was no hand to steady the wheel. The vehicle started to drift off course, swerving into the middle lane, which caused a driver overtaking to take evasive action. He moved into the third lane and blasted his horn in rebuke, but there was no one in the lorry's cab to hear him.

The truck continued to veer to the right, forcing other drivers to perform drastic avoiding manoeuvres, but the worst was yet to come. Despite slowing down to around half its original speed of sixty miles per hour, it crashed through the central reservation and into the path of oncoming traffic on the northbound carriageway. This was just before reaching one of the many bridges that spanned the motorway.

Immediately, chaos ensued. An Audi, travelling at over ninety miles per hour in the fast lane as the driver rushed to get home after a very important meeting in London, never stood a chance. He collided head-on with the lorry and was killed instantly. Several following vehicles crashed into the wreckage, with a few bursting into flames, resulting in a scene of pure destruction. The collisions caused the lorry to veer back towards the central reservation where it eventually came to a stop when it crashed into one of the pillars that supported the bridge.

In the space of a few seconds, Britain had just suffered its worst motorway pile-up in years.

While all this was happening, a few miles away in the police station of the local market town, DI Hannah Benson was interviewing a suspect in a small interrogation room. Thirty-two years old, she was in the prime of her life and cut a trim, fit figure, topped by her short blonde hair. The man opposite her at the table was of similar age, but significantly less well kept. The cheap white Lonsdale t-shirt he was wearing was stained and had small holes starting to form in it. He also looked as if he hadn't washed for a couple of days and he certainly hadn't shaved.

The room wasn't air-conditioned and there were beads of sweat beginning to form on his forehead, merely adding to the nervous vibes he was giving off. That wasn't all the man was exuding. In the warm summer weather, it was apparent he hadn't been acquainted with any deodorant for a while.

There was little doubt about the man's guilt in Hannah's eyes. Thirty-three-year-old Harry Richards was a convicted sex offender who had served time and recently been let out of jail on licence. Hannah's opinion was that he shouldn't have been let out at all given his record, but it wasn't her job to make the rules; she just enforced them.

"I didn't do anything," he insisted.

"I've got two witnesses who say otherwise. Lifeguards at the outside swimming pool."

"I was just adjusting myself. They get very sticky on a hot day like this."

"You were not adjusting yourself. You were flashing your aroused genitals at a group of women in front of the ladies' changing room. It's all been caught on camera, so there is no point trying to deny it."

"I demand to see a solicitor."

"One has been called," she said. "But I doubt it will do you much good. You've got form, as one of my predecessors in this role used to say."

"What if I say I identify as a woman? Can't do anything, then, can you?"

"Your attire, stubble, and general appearance would suggest otherwise," replied Hannah.

A knock on the door interrupted the interview, and a young female officer who had been observing the interview opened it to inquire as to the cause of the interruption. Turning back towards the table, she motioned for Hannah to come over.

"What is it, Constable Stevens?"

"We've got a situation," said the younger woman in a low voice. "You're needed out front."

"Fine," said Hannah, annoyed at the interruption. "Keep an eye on him."

She suspended the interview and went out to the front desk where her colleague, Adrian Johnson, was being harangued by a familiar figure. It was a local farmer named Arthur Tuddenham. On seeing him, she was annoyed. Surely she hadn't been dragged out of the meeting just to deal with yet another one of his endless complaints?

Despite the clement weather, Arthur was wearing heavy-duty clothing, including a pair of muddy boots, thick brown trousers, a waxed Barbour jacket and a green flat cap. This outfit never seemed to vary, no matter what time of year Hannah encountered him. And she ran into him a lot. He was always turning up at the station moaning about everything from errant ramblers to the local doggers, who he claimed were having gangbangs behind one of his barns.

"It's no good you saying you've got an emergency," said Arthur. "I want to know what you're going to do about these cattle rustlers. I've had two cows go missing today in broad daylight! Do you have any idea how much those Friesians cost? Over two grand! Probably more like three now, what with all this inflation. And are the supermarkets going to pay me more for my milk to reflect this? Are they f…"

"I'm sorry, Mr Tuddenham, but like I said we've got an emergency and we are very short-staffed," said Adrian, interrupting him before he could utter the obscenity. "If you come back tomorrow, I promise we'll give it our full attention."

"That's bloody typical of you lot," said Arthur, as he made his way to the door. "Wash your hands of it, as usual. This would never have happened in Kent's day."

5

"Very little ever happened in Kent's day," said Hannah. "As Sergeant Johnson said, we'll deal with it tomorrow. Oh, and I do hope you haven't parked that tractor of yours across the exit again. I'll issue you with a ticket if you have."

Arthur quickened his pace towards the door, suggesting that he had indeed been amiss in his choice of parking spot. With him gone, Adrian briefed Hannah on the news of the pileup on the M40. The emergency services were already on the scene but it looked very bad and they needed more senior officers to assist with the investigation into the cause of the crash.

She had been scheduled to clock off at six which was in less than an hour, but it went with the territory of the job that she couldn't always be home on time to see her three-year-old daughter, Jess. Most of the time she lived the life of a single parent. She was in a relationship with a man called Peter who travelled in time and he was currently away. He wouldn't return until the following year.

Fortunately Hannah had a good support network, and at that moment one of her closest friends, Kaylee, was taking care of Jess for her. Kaylee had recently returned from her final year at university and was more than happy to lend a hand.

After making a couple of calls in her office confirming that things were in a bad way on the motorway, Hannah agreed to go and assist with the investigation. This meant that she would not be able to spend any more time interviewing Harry Richards. Consequently, she made the necessary arrangements to have him put in a holding cell for the night and left Adrian in charge.

What she saw when she reached the location of the accident was not a pretty sight. The lorry was blocking part of the northern carriageway, along with at least six other vehicles that had crashed into it. It was apparent from the body bags being loaded into ambulances that there had been fatalities, and the fire crews were still busy cutting people out of a couple of cars. She had no idea at this stage if they were alive or dead.

The road had been closed in both directions and other than the sounds of the equipment being used on the stricken vehicles, there was an eerie silence, despite the large number of emergency vehicles in attendance.

"Hannah," called a familiar voice from close to the lorry's cab. "Over here."

She recognised the voice immediately. It was that of DCI Dan Bradley, a veteran of the force from Oxford with over three decades of experience. He was close to retirement and a little too old-school for her liking, reminding her of her old boss, Richard Kent. Nevertheless, his presence in the hellhole around her was a reassuring one.

"What the hell happened here, Dan?" she asked.

"That's what we're trying to find out," he said. "It appears that this lorry veered across the road and broke through the central reservation."

"Any theories about why?"

"Well, it can't be to do with the weather. I did see something like this, over thirty years ago not long after this stretch first opened, but it was in the dark, in thick fog and icy conditions."

"Could the driver have had a heart attack? Or have fallen asleep at the wheel? It does happen," said Hannah, trying to come up with some other explanation.

"Well, that's the oddest thing. We can't find him."

"He's done a runner?"

"I don't see how he could have. I mean look at the state of it."

The front of the lorry was completely smashed in where it had hit the pillar. It was hard to imagine anyone inside being in any fit state to flee the scene.

"I see what you mean. Thank goodness that pillar is made of solid stuff. I don't want to even think about what might have happened if the bridge had come down," she said, noticing the cameras on top of the bridge before adding, "is there any footage from those cameras up there?"

"They're checking it now."

"There will be dashcam film from within the cab too," she said. "Maybe that could shed some light on what happened."

"Maybe," said Dan. "But I still find it incredible that he's not in the cab. The firemen who investigated said it was basically impossible. Even if he wasn't injured, which would have been miraculous, the door was so badly mangled, he wouldn't have been able to open it."

"What do we know about him?"

"Jake Rogers, aged forty-nine, with over twenty-five years of experience driving heavy goods vehicles. Clean licence, clean record, family man, no known medical problems."

"Sounds as reliable as they come," said Hannah.

"He was," replied Dan. "So I am racking my brains for an explanation of why or how this could have happened. And he can't tell us, not until we find him."

"If we find him."

"What do you mean? He must be here somewhere. I already told you, he cannot possibly have got away."

"Then where is he?"

Dan just looked at her, with a thoughtful expression on his face. It was a mystery, which put him in mind of some similar unexplained disappearances, way back in 1992, when he had been a young officer in Oxford. Most of those people had reappeared eventually but it had been a strange few weeks, for which he had never come up with any sort of adequate explanation.

The clean-up operation took many hours, extending long into the night. Hannah got away at about 10pm and when she returned home she found Kaylee curled up on the sofa watching a drama series on the television.

"Kaylee, I'm so sorry," she said. "Thank you so much for staying, I can't tell you how grateful I am."

"Hey, that's OK," said Kaylee, sitting up and letting her long blonde hair fall loose across her shoulders. "I didn't have anywhere special to be tonight. Charlie is out with Josh having a few drinks in Oxford to celebrate their graduation. It's the first chance they've had since we got back from Bristol."

"Did Jess go off to sleep alright?"

"Yes, she's been as good as gold. I bathed her about seven, read her a story, and she was asleep not long after. Is everything OK? I saw on the news about the crash; it looked awful."

"It was," she said. "I don't know about you, but I could do with a drink. Do you fancy cracking open a bottle of wine? I could do with a glass after the day I've had."

"I won't say no," said Kaylee. "What have you got?"

"There's a nice drop of chardonnay in the fridge. I popped it in there this morning before I left. I so much prefer white wine when the weather is hot like this, don't you? After the summer we've had, we should make the most of this weather while it lasts."

"I like white, but Charlie always insists on red," said Kaylee. "Between you and me, I think he fancies himself as a bit of a wine snob."

"Peter's a bit like that too," said Hannah. "From what little I remember. God, I miss him. How many years are we going to have to be apart like this? It gets harder every time he goes away."

"At least you have Jess. And all of us, of course."

"Where would I be without you?" said Hannah. "Come on, let's get this open and go and sit out on the decking. It's lovely at this time of night."

Over the next hour, Hannah felt the stresses of the day melt away as she and Kaylee chatted away over the wine. Try as she might, Hannah often found it difficult to switch off from work, particularly after harrowing scenes such as those she had witnessed today. Thankfully, tonight the younger woman's company really helped.

Unfortunately, her respite from the rigours of work was to be short-lived. After a few hours of welcome sleep, her phone rang just before 7 o'clock the following morning. On the other end of the line was a panicked officer who had been on overnight duty at the station. He was calling her with the last thing she wanted to hear.

In less than an hour, she was in the station demanding answers.

"What do you mean, he's escaped, Sergeant Smith?"

11

"I mean just that," said the man in front of her, with a bewildered look on his face."

"When? How?"

"I don't know."

"You're meant to check on him every thirty minutes. Did you?"

"Of course I did. And he was there, sleeping, all night."

"When did you last see him?"

"About six-thirty. Then I checked again at seven and the cell was empty."

"I want to see for myself," said Hannah, so she and Sergeant Smith headed for the cells so she could examine the scene in detail.

"I don't understand this," she said. "There's no sign of any damage to the door or the lock. Or the window, come to that."

"Maybe he had a key?"

"From where?" asked Hannah. "And even so, how would he have got through the security door?"

"Or someone sprung him?"

"Without you or anyone else seeing? I take it you have checked the CCTV?"

"Yes, and no one's been in or out the whole time. It's a classic locked room mystery, isn't it?" said Smith. "It reminds me of a show I used to watch with my dad when I was a kid about this oddball who lived in a windmill. He used to solve stuff like this all the time."

"Do you mean *Jonathan Creek*?" asked Hannah.

"Yes, that's the chap. Maybe we should send for him, eh, boss?"

"This isn't a matter for flippancy, Sergeant. A prisoner in our care has escaped. Do you have any idea how much trouble that puts me in? And you, come to that. We're not popular with the top brass up here as it is. The commissioner has had it in for us ever since he fell out with Kent a few years ago."

"Ah, yes, the dreaded Gideon Summerfield."

"Please, don't even mention his name. It sends shivers down my spine every time I hear it."

"Maybe we should keep it quiet, while we look for him?" suggested Smith.

"That is the last thing we should do! It will make things even worse. I need to submit a report right away. If I don't then it will look like we're trying to cover it up. In the meantime, get Johnson down here and organise a search."

She was so stressed by the situation, that it didn't immediately occur to her to connect the previous day's incident with Jake Rogers to this latest disappearance. She was more

13

concerned with the dressing down she was going to get from above and it wasn't long in coming. Summerfield wasn't known for mincing his words and he gave it to her with both barrels on a video call.

"No, we cannot keep it quiet, Benson. We've got a convicted sex offender on the loose. If he assaults someone and it turned out we didn't warn the public, our reputation will be in the gutter! Which it practically already is in your town, thanks to years of ineptitude from that dinosaur Kent."

She was left in the unenviable position of having to issue a press release, as well as social media statements, informing the local populace of the escape. This, as always, did not go down well. She hated issuing tweets from the official local police force account because all that ever came back in response was ridicule and abuse.

She didn't even bother looking at the replies anymore but was assured by Smith that they were almost universal in their condemnation. They varied from the relatively minor accusations of incompetence to much more sinister allegations suggesting everything the police did was part of some sort of global masterplan to enslave the people. As far as she was concerned, she was just doing her job.

To make matters worse Johnson, having agreed to come back to the station to assist, never showed up. Dealing with an escaped prisoner was hard enough, without having to chase errant staff as well. It was annoying because he was usually so reliable.

It was her second stressful day in a row, but the worst, by far, was still to come.

Chapter Two
July 2023

"Never again," said Josh, as he rummaged around in the fridge of his student flat, desperately looking for some orange juice to ease his hangover. There was none. Typical. He had tried labelling his stuff, but it was to no avail.

"And there was me thinking sharing a student house would be fun," he added. "It's been a bloody nightmare."

"Yeah, well, you're not technically a student anymore, are you?" said Charlie, from the sofa in the open-plan apartment where he had crashed the night. "Neither of us are. Now the grownup stuff begins. Speaking of which, perhaps we ought to adopt a more mature approach to alcohol. I'm seriously hanging, here."

"That's good coming from you," said Josh. "I told you we should have gone home after the pub shut, but you insisted on going to a club."

"It seemed like a good idea at the time," said Charlie. "But I hadn't seen you since before our finals and now it is all done and dusted we had every reason to celebrate."

"Yes, well now you're back in Oxford I daresay we'll see each other more often. A shame you went to Bristol, really. It's hardly got the same kudos as Oxbridge, has it?"

"I suppose not. Have you got anything to eat?" asked Charlie.

"Chance would be a fine thing. There's nothing in this fridge at all. Thieves and vagabonds, the people I've been living with, the lot of them."

"I didn't have that problem in Bristol. Kaylee and I had our own place."

"Yeah, well you wouldn't have been able to afford that in Oxford. I read a report the other day that said we've got the highest cost of living in Britain here."

"No wonder everyone's been nicking your food, then."

"Thing is, I'm the only one still here! All the others have gone home and I need to be out of here this weekend. Emma was the last to leave, she went yesterday. I reckon it was her that emptied the fridge before she left. I had some bacon and eggs in there I was going to cook this morning. That's gone. So much for her claiming to be a vegan. Thank God I'll never have to see her again. It's been a year of hell sharing a house with her."

"I take it you didn't get on?"

"No. She accused me of being arrogant. Me! Arrogant! Can you believe it?"

"I'm saying nothing," said Charlie, who had known Josh for a long time. "But not to worry, we can go to a café in town. And after that, I've got to get back home to Kaylee. She was babysitting for Hannah last night."

"You two couldn't be more like an old married couple if you tried," said Josh. "Still, moving back into your mum's place must have cramped your style a bit. Is that a temporary or a permanent arrangement?"

"Hopefully only until we both get jobs but the price of rent around here is shocking, as you well know. Still, it could be worse. We could be living at her parents' place. You know what her sister's like."

"Ah, yes, the delightful Olivia. How could two siblings be so different?"

"Indeed. Anyway, like I said, it won't be long. I've got all sorts of leads on LinkedIn."

"What about Kaylee? What opportunities are there for someone with a degree in meteorology? Weather girl? There can't be that many vacancies for them."

"You'd be surprised how many people the MET office employs," said Charlie. "It's not just about standing in front of a screen pointing at a map, you know. But whatever she decides to do, there is no need to hurry into anything. We want to make the most of this summer before we get tied down to full-time jobs for the next forty years."

"Fair enough. I suppose we had better get our acts together. I need to pack up the rest of my stuff today. Whatever I've got left, anyway. I wouldn't put it past that Emma to have nicked more than just the contents of the fridge."

After a slap-up breakfast at Charlie's favourite café on Broad Street, they went their separate ways and Josh made his way back to the college at which he had been an undergraduate for the past three years.

His destination was Professor Anthony Hamilton's lab, a place he had been frequenting during the past year. Hamilton was not only his tutor but also a passionate scientist, specialising in experiments with tachyonic particles. He had been trying to make a breakthrough in this discipline for many years in the hope of proving that time travel was possible. So far, he had been unsuccessful.

His obsession was right up Josh's alley, as he had first-hand experience of time travel using a time bubble a few years previously. And that wasn't his only time travelling encounter. About a year and a half ago he had run into a man at Cheltenham races who had claimed to be a time traveller and asked him to meet him on a specific date in 1990. This was a peculiar request considering it was currently 2023 but he couldn't doubt the man's knowledge. He had known the result of every race on the card in advance. This encounter inspired him to get involved with his tutor's work.

It was rare for the members of the time bubble team to share their knowledge outside the group but Josh had convinced them to allow him to confide in Professor Hamilton about his experiences. During his final year of study, he had found himself spending increasing amounts of time in the lab, discussing theories, and talking about whether they could pool their resources and make controlled time travel a reality.

Sometimes he felt as if Hamilton were holding back on him and knew more about the subject than he was letting on. Sometimes, usually after a few drinks, he would make outlandish claims, such as on one occasion when he was adamant that he had seen a dinosaur in Oxford in 1992. He often backtracked on these in the cold light of the following day, claiming it was just a joke, but it was always difficult to tell with Hamilton.

His mentor had more than a hint of the classic mad professor look about him, with his wild white hair and beard. Consequently, many years ago the students had bestowed the nickname Gandalf upon him. Despite pushing retirement age, he was still a lively figure and when he got exceptionally excited about something he became very animated and his Scottish accent grew stronger.

Josh wasn't sure how long he had been at the college, but as with numerous ageing Oxford academics, it appeared as though he had been there forever and would be there forever. Such was the timeless nature of life at the university.

He was clearly in fine fettle when Josh entered the lab on this sunny Saturday, rushing over and enthusiastically shaking hands as if they were being acquainted for the first time.

"Josh, my boy, an absolute delight to see you! I take it the finals went well?"

"I believe they did," said Josh, assured that they had. He was, even if he said so himself, somewhat of a mathematical genius.

"Never in doubt, my dear fellow, you were always going to pass with flying colours. I trust you have been celebrating in the appropriate style. If you don't mind me saying, you look a little rough around the edges this morning. Take it from one who knows! Perhaps a hair of the dog might be in order. I'm sure I've got a drop of Glenmorangie knocking around here somewhere."

"It's been a pretty wild week," admitted Josh, who was indeed still feeling a little ropey, despite the large breakfast. "I think I'll pass on the whisky, though, if you don't mind. It's a little early for that."

"As long as you've been enjoying yourself, that's the main thing. You've earned it. But it's time to think of the future now, laddie. And a very bright future it's going to be for you, too!"

"You seem very confident of that," said Josh.

"Oh, I am, my boy, I am. And it all begins right here, today. You see, I have a little proposal for you. An offer you can't refuse, you could say!"

This wasn't entirely unexpected. Hamilton had dropped several hints about what he had in mind in recent weeks and Josh had already guessed what was coming. But he didn't say anything to spoil Hamilton's big reveal.

"Tell me more," he said, with a curious look on his face as he tried to make out that he didn't have a clue what Hamilton was talking about.

"I've been very impressed with you, young man, and the help you've given me this past year has been invaluable. Now that you've finished your degree, I can't bear to think of your talents going to waste in some unworthy institution elsewhere. If that rogue Garfunkel at Cambridge got his mitts on you I'd never forgive myself. So how do you fancy coming to work here, with me? We'll carry on our time travel work and you can study for a postgraduate degree with a view to taking on some lecturing as part of your future role."

"What can I say?" said Josh. "It's a very tempting offer."

"And a very lucrative one," said Hamilton. "You'll be starting on a minimum of sixty thousand, rising rapidly thereafter. We look after our own here. And that's very much what I see you as. This is not just a job, it's a family. I can't go on forever, and I need to know my life's work is in safe hands."

"You see me as your prodigy?"

"Absolutely, dear boy! I have no heir and I've been waiting for years for a student to come along with a mind to challenge my own. I was beginning to lose hope, but then you arrived. What do you say?"

Josh paused for a moment, wrinkling up his face into a pensive façade as if he was giving careful consideration to the proposal. In truth, he was doing no such thing. He had anticipated the offer and it was everything he wanted. He loved being at the college, and having continued access to the lab and all the other facilities would enable him to continue pursuing his long-term goal. One day he would create a device that would enable him to create time bubbles like the one he had found five years ago.

After letting the professor sweat a bit, he announced, "I'd be delighted! Now I just need to find somewhere to live. The lease on my student house runs out this weekend."

"Wonderful, my boy, wonderful," said Hamilton, enthusiastically grabbing Josh's hand and pumping it with a way over-the-top handshake. "You won't regret it! And don't worry about the accommodation. The university owns plenty of desirable dwellings in the city. As I said before, we look after our own!"

As Josh's career prospects were on the rise, his ex-girlfriend Lauren was seeing hers heading in the opposite direction. She too was on the move, but for the wrong reasons. The two of them had been an on-off item for a couple of years during sixth form and his first year at university, but neither of them was committed and eventually agreed to stay friends but go their separate ways.

She had stayed in the city, sharing a flat with another girl, but the rent was exorbitant. Despite working all the hours she could get, she still struggled to get by, and now she was completely out of options. She had recently been let go by the beautician she had been working for. Her boss claimed it was due to lack of work but she knew the truth was that they just didn't want her. If she was brutally honest with herself, she had to admit that she didn't want them either. The job had been one long disappointment.

It had been marginally better than her attempt to be a hairdresser, but not much. Rather than styling the hair of the rich and famous, which was what she had envisaged, that job had turned out to be mostly listening to old ladies rambling on about their ailments.

She was young and needed a job where she could meet and interact with people her own age. Her favourite thing was bar work, but that was unreliable and didn't pay enough for her to make her way. Eventually, broke and with the credit card debts mounting up, she had no choice but to bite the bullet and go home to her mother, Patricia.

It was a reunion she was dreading. Quite simply, she and her mother just did not get along. Lauren had a free-spirited nature and enjoyed living life on her own terms, something which attracted maternal disapproval. She found her mother to be strict and overly serious. If she had ever known how to have fun, it was a long time in the past. She was also very sceptical of people and institutions, especially the media and the government. It was all she ever went on about.

Lauren could sort of sympathise with that; she was no fan of authority herself, but did her mother have to bang on and on about it all the time? She had never seen her laugh, or barely even smile. Virtually every conversation they had had since she had been a young teenager had ended up in an argument. There was no father to smooth the situation. He was long gone.

Occasionally her mother made a token effort, asking if she wanted to go somewhere with her or watch TV with her, but it was always utterly boring places like garden centres or equally tedious programmes about gardening and home makeovers. Or even worse, endless YouTube videos about the latest conspiracy theories.

Lauren had come back from Oxford on the bus, lugging a heavy suitcase that contained pretty much all her worldly goods. It wasn't much to show for three years in the city. The bus driver had been quite young and friendly and she had tried flirting with him to take her mind off her impending return home. Smiling from her pretty, round face, she flicked at the edge of her black bob of hair with her fingers as she waited for him to give out her change. He smiled back and then made a point of flashing his wedding ring at her. It just wasn't her day.

Back at the house, she pulled out the front door key that she hadn't used in over three years, took a deep breath, and went to open the door. But she didn't need the key. The door was already unlocked.

That meant her mother was at home. It was to be expected, she supposed, with it being Saturday lunchtime. She had rung home earlier in the week to give advance warning she was coming, which had not been well received. There had been much moaning about not having enough food in the house or the bed being made up. As usual, it quickly escalated into a row after Lauren suggested that four days should be ample time to go shopping and sort out the sheets. It was obvious she was not wanted there and she prayed this would be a temporary arrangement.

She could hear that the television was on and made her way through to the darkened living room, where her mother was watching TV with the curtains closed. She barely looked up as Lauren came in.

"Oh, you're here then," she said.

"Obviously," replied Lauren, looking to see what her mother was watching. It was some bloke in a small room with various pieces of memorabilia from well-known science fiction shows and movies displayed on shelves behind him. He was talking very fast and was clearly excited about something.

"Who's this?" she asked.

"That's Mystic Mick!" she said. "You must know who Mystic Mick is!"

"Should I?"

"Of course! He reveals the truths the real media won't touch. You won't get this on the BBC news."

"I don't watch the BBC news. I don't watch any news. I don't see the point. I'd rather just get on and live my life."

"Of course you would," said Patricia. "All you care about is where your next drink and fuck is coming from."

"What a dreadful thing to say to your only daughter."

"It's true, though, isn't it? If it doesn't come in a bottle or a pair of trousers you're not interested."

"Just because you're past it. If you ever had it."

"I was young once, you know."

"Yeah, about a century ago. So what's Mystic Mick on about? It's not the moon landings again, is it?"

"No, it's about these people going missing. You should watch it."

"Must I?"

"Indulge me. I am letting you live here, after all."

"This is my childhood home. What parent would turn their only child away? Actually, don't answer that."

"Just listen," said Patricia, reaching for the remote and turning up the volume.

"And they haven't said a word on the news about it," said Mystic Mick. "But I'm telling you now, the driver of that truck was nowhere to be found after the accident. Now you tell me, how can a driver in the middle of all this carnage, simply disappear?"

The video cut to a screenshot of the aftermath of the chaos on the M40.

"I tell you, he can't. Which makes me question whether this even was an accident. What are they hiding? And he isn't the only one. Take a look at this woman."

The view switched again to a still of a professional-looking lady in a smart business suit, aged around forty.

"This is Lorraine Green, a newly appointed board member at one of Britain's biggest high street banks. According to inside sources, she excused herself yesterday afternoon during a meeting break, went into the ladies' room and never came out. CCTV confirmed this. Where did she go? They were on the thirty-third floor and there was no other way out. So what happened to her? Her husband and young children are beside themselves with worry. And well they should be. Did the state have something against Mrs Green? Did she know something they wanted buried? These questions need to be answered!"

"For God's sake, Mum, you don't really believe all this rubbish, do you? It's a lovely afternoon, the first decent spell of weather we've had for weeks. Why are you sitting in here watching this with the curtains closed?"

"It's not rubbish," insisted Patricia. "Anyway, it's my house and my television. I'll do what I want."

"Of course you will," replied Lauren. "You always have."

She turned, left the room, and headed up the stairs. Up in her old teenage bedroom, she found a quilt cover, pillowcase and sheet neatly folded on top of her bed. Her mother hadn't even bothered to make it up.

As for the rest of the room, there was not an inch of spare floor place. It appeared that her mother had taken to using it as a storeroom and had stockpiled it to the ceiling with enough food to feed an army. There were hundreds of tins of fruit, tuna, and ham, along with powdered milk, and countless other foodstuffs. There were also dozens of large bottles of water, the gallon-sized ones you often found in supermarkets in holiday resorts.

So much for the conversation on the phone earlier in the week when she claimed she didn't have enough food! It was a wonder the floorboards hadn't caved in.

Why would her mother ever need so much stuff, and why would she fill her room with it? It wasn't even worth trying to figure out the workings of her disturbed mind. All Lauren knew was that the sooner she got a job and got out of this place, the better.

Chapter Three
July 2023

Kaylee had once again agreed to look after Jess for the day, which helped Hannah out as the nursery she normally went to wasn't open at the weekend. With Jess taken care of, Hannah could concentrate on spending the day addressing some of the issues that had arisen over the past twenty-four hours.

The search for both Harry Richards and Jake Rogers had yielded no results. Neither of them had returned to their respective homes, and no one had seen them. The situation left Jake's family in Oxford distraught and seeking answers. His wife, Amanda, was actively seeking publicity through social media, local journalists, and the Oxford police to raise awareness. She was convinced that there had to be someone, somewhere, who could shed some light on his disappearance.

A press conference had been called for 2pm which was going to be broadcast live on the BBC's rolling news channel. Hannah was not required to attend as the investigation was being handled by the Oxford police. She had been in touch with Dan Bradley and knew he would be addressing the press as he had been put in charge. Alone in her office, she accessed the BBC website via her laptop and waited for the conference to begin.

But begin, it did not. Leading up to the scheduled start time, there had been a banner scrolling along the bottom of the screen announcing the upcoming event. Then, just before the hour, it disappeared. The presenter made no further reference to the story, and a quick switch to other news channels revealed a similar lack of coverage. What was happening?

These same questions were being asked in Oxford. Several journalists, both national and local, had assembled for the conference which had been hastily arranged in a local school hall. Among them was Seema Mistry, a local BBC reporter who worked for Radio Oxford. She, along with the others, had taken seats in the hall, where she had got chatting to a reporter from Sky News. Between them, they had been speculating as to what might have happened to Jake Rogers and agreeing between them which questions they were going to ask.

The situation was perplexing, and in the lengthy delay some of the suggestions were beginning to veer towards the sort of content Mystic Mick had been putting out on his channel.

Finally, at 2.20, Dan Bradley emerged onto the stage to speak to the assembled throng. Of Jake's wife, whom they had been expecting to give an emotional speech, there was no sign.

"I'm very sorry to have wasted all of your time, but I regret to announce that there will be no press conference today."

He looked out at the disgruntled faces of the audience, who let out their disapproval via a chorus of muttering, assorted groans, and a very audible "fuck's sake" from Keith Diamond, an infamous tabloid journalist who used to host a popular talk show on ChatFM before he was sacked for his controversial opinions.

"In addition, due to the sensitive nature of this story, and under emergency powers, it is my duty to inform you all that as of this moment there is a total news blackout on this story. This also applies to any other story regarding unexplained disappearances. Your respective organisations will already be receiving new guidelines from OFCOM and you will be expected to adhere to them. Failure to do so will invoke swift penalties. That is all."

Without further ado he left the stage, retreating behind a curtain where a very senior civil servant was waiting, out of sight of the journalists. Dan recognised the wiry figure, with his John Lennon glasses, short cropped hair, and trademark ginger beard, right away.

Dominic Campbell had been instrumental in influencing government policy for some years. He was viewed with suspicion by a large portion of the population, particularly those who suspected civil servants and spin doctors had far too much power to manipulate public opinion via various dubious practices. If those people were privy to the conversation taking place now, they would take it as an endorsement of their suspicions.

"Good work, Dan, that's exactly what we needed you to say," said Dominic.

"I still don't understand why," said Dan, who was feeling distinctly uncomfortable about the situation. There was something distinctly cloak and dagger about all of this and he didn't like it.

"Of course, you don't. But let me worry about the why. You just concentrate on the what."

"I'm sorry, but that's not good enough. You cancel the conference at the last minute, spirit that poor woman off to goodness knows where, and expect me not to ask any questions?"

He was referring to an incident backstage before he had addressed the journalist. There, he had witnessed Jake's wife being led away by uniformed officers on the pretext of some security issue. He had not seen her since.

"Mrs Rogers needed to vacate the premises for her own safety. Don't worry, she'll be taken care of. All you need to do is keep things everything running smoothly while we deal with the important stuff behind the scenes. There is to be no discussion of this matter with anyone, do I make myself clear? The public is to be kept in the dark. Nothing to see here, as I believe you people say in the movies."

"And you think they are just going to accept that? Do you think they won't talk amongst themselves about these disappearances? It's not just this Rogers guy that's gone missing. There are many more."

"The public has a massive capacity for self-delusion. We've pulled the wool over their eyes plenty of times before. You could say we've become experts at it. Did you know that we have a whole department made up of psychologists dedicated to it? The people will believe what we want them to believe. And they'll act accordingly. The trick is to dupe them into thinking that they are coming to their own autonomous decisions. Whereas what we have really done is steer them down the exact route we want them to go. Like herding cattle onto a truck."

"That doesn't sit well with me at all."

"I don't care how it sits with you, Dan. I just need you to do your job. That's not going to be a problem, is it? Because I'm very good at making problems go away when I need to. I think you know what I'm talking about, don't you?"

Dominic fixed Dan with a cold, hard stare, the chill of the threat coursing into the senior police officer's bones.

"Yes," said Dan reluctantly. He despised this jumped-up little prick, but to defy him would have been on a par with declaring Catholicism to be the one true religion in front of Henry VIII. It might not result in him having his head chopped off in front of a baying mob, but he did not doubt that Dominic had the means to effect a more modern and discreet equivalent.

"Oh, and if you get any more calls asking you to investigate missing persons? Ignore them. Your priority is to maintain law and order."

"And that's it?"

Dominic declared, "That's it," before striding out of the room and towards the rear of the building. A car with tinted windows was already stationed there, ready to transport him back to Westminster. He slid into the back seat and exhaled a deep sigh of relief. Maintaining an image of complete control in public was crucial to Dominic and he was confident he had projected himself effectively to Dan Bradley. Now that he was safely concealed in the car he could relax.

In truth, although he relished exuding an air of privileged insight, he was just as clueless about what was going on as everybody else. It was frustrating, but hopefully he would get to the bottom of it before things got out of hand. If the disappearances were due to higher powers, either at home or abroad, the perpetrators hadn't communicated their intentions to him. That irked him. He was more worried about being left out of the loop than about the nature of the threat. Nothing went on in Westminster he didn't know about and he intended things to stay that way.

Dan was equally frustrated. He had been left with the impression that something big was going on and that he wasn't important enough to be a party to it. Unlike Dominic, he didn't have the luxury of someone to spirit him away in a darkened car, which meant he was going to have to try to make his way out of the school without being accosted by inquisitive journalists. As he pondered how best to vacate the premises unseen, his phone began to vibrate in his pocket. When he took it out and saw that it was Hannah calling he answered right away. He always had time for her.

"Dan, what's happened to the press conference? There's nothing on any of the channels."

"News blackout. We've been told that we're not allowed to talk about it."

"But why? We're dealing with missing people here, not some threat to national security."

"For all we know, that's exactly what it is," said Dan. "I can't say any more except that there was a very senior official here earlier and I was told in no uncertain terms to keep my mouth shut. I've no idea what's going on, but I have a strong suspicion that we aren't going to see any of those missing people again anytime soon."

"OK. You'll let me know if you hear anything, won't you?" asked Hannah.

"I will. Looking on the bright side, you will probably be off the hook now regarding your missing sex offender. I imagine that will fall under the remit of the blackout too."

They ended the call, and Hannah headed back out to the front desk where Sergeant Smith was now on duty.

"Still no news on Harry Richards?" she asked.

"Nothing, I'm afraid. I'm not sure what else we can do; we've made a comprehensive search of all the places he usually goes."

Hannah agreed. There was nothing to be done so she decided to head home for the day, leaving Smith with instructions to call her if there were any developments.

Back at the school, Dan Bradley had managed to slip out of a gate at the rear of the school playing field with the assistance of the caretaker. It led onto a quiet housing estate, off the

Abingdon Road. Just as he was congratulating himself on evading the journalists, one of them stepped out from behind a bush and challenged him.

"What the hell was that about?" demanded Seema, who was the last person that Dan wanted to see. In recent years, he had found that investigative journalists had become less pushy than they had been at the beginning of his career. They certainly didn't have the free rein that they had enjoyed back in the 1980s. But Seema was the exception to the rule. The young Asian woman was like a dog with a bone when she got her teeth into something and wouldn't let go. He almost admired her for it in a way, despite the trouble she had caused him since she burst onto the scene a few years before. But this time, he was going to have to convince her to drop it.

"I'm as much in the dark as you are, Seema. There is nothing I can tell you."

"Can't or won't?" she replied, following Dan who had started walking away through the estate. All he wanted to do now was navigate his way back to where he had parked his car, on a side street out of view of the front of the school. Then he could get away from her.

"Can't. And even if I could, there's nothing you could publish anyway, so why are you pursuing this? I'm sure you've already been told this by your superiors."

"I have. The station manager from Radio Oxford texted me while you were on the stage. But I still want to know to satisfy my curiosity."

Dan sighed with exasperation, not only at her persistence but at his lack of understanding as to what was going on.

"Look, I know as much as you do. People are disappearing. No one knows why. Orders have come down from on high making it clear that there is to be a total blackout on discussion of this. Believe me, I've been doing this job a long time and I know when to keep my mouth shut."

"Why? Afraid of the truth? Or what might happen to you?"

"Look, Seema, you're young, you don't have my life experience and you need to learn when to keep your mouth shut too. If you pursue this you're going to be stirring up a whole lot of trouble for yourself."

"You know, I am sick of people of your generation assuming that because I'm young I don't know anything. It's patronising. I'm not some wet behind the ears kid. For your information, I'm closer to thirty than twenty and I've been a journalist in some shape or form for over ten years. I know how the world works."

"Then why are we having this conversation? The BBC won't let you broadcast anything to do with this, and if you put it out on a podcast or a blog somewhere, your career will be finished."

"Do you think I don't know that? This isn't business, it's personal. I'm not publishing anything anywhere. I just want to know what's going on. I have an enquiring mind, a rarity these days, I know, but there it is."

"And I'm telling you again, I don't know," said Dan, as with relief he turned a corner to see his car parked ahead of him.

"Fine," said Seema. "If you can't help me, I will find someone who will."

"Good luck with that, then," said Dan. "Because I don't think even the top brass know what's going on. All I know is, if it keeps happening, they aren't going to be able to cover it up forever."

He unlocked his BMW with the fob, climbed in and drove away. Seema watched him go, disappointed that the conversation hadn't yielded any answers, but determined to find out more.

Meanwhile, Hannah had called Kaylee to let her know she was on her way home. It had turned out to be another warm and sunny afternoon, and when Kaylee took the call, she and Jess were out in the back garden making the most of it.

At the age of three, Jess was incredibly inquisitive about the world. As she and Kaylee sat on a red and green tartan picnic rug on the rear lawn, the young child was bombarding the woman with questions about everything that caught her eye. Right now, the topic was ladybirds, of which the warm weather had brought an influx. Jess was fascinated by the two small red insects that were currently crawling around on her arm.

"Why has this one got two spots and this one got four?" she asked.

"Oh, that tells you how old they are," said Kaylee. "Every year, they get a new one on their birthday."

Kaylee knew this wasn't the real reason. She didn't know the correct answer to the girl's question, so like many adults talking to small children, she came up with a fun answer. It didn't do any harm. It was all part of the imagination that came with the innocence and joy of childhood, like the tooth fairy and Father Christmas. At Jess's age, all things were still possible.

"Why haven't I got three spots?" asked Jess, taking the conversation to the next logical step that her developing three-year-old mind had led her to.

"Because you're not a ladybird," said Kaylee. "You're a human."

"Why am I a human?"

This was a more difficult question, which Kaylee struggled to come up with an answer to.

"Because your parents are humans," she answered, after a pause.

"Why am I me?"

This was starting to get tricky. Kaylee decided to change the subject.

"It's very warm today, isn't it? Are you thirsty?"

"Yes."

"Would you like a drink?"

"In my blue sippy cup?"

"Of course."

"Can you get a drink for the ladybirds? They must be hot too."

"I most certainly will," said Kaylee, humouring her.

She got up from the blanket and walked onto the small patio area at the rear of the house. It was a red-brick, terraced dwelling, typical of the sort of homes built in the late nineteenth century. It was a long, thin house and the garden was the same, just a few yards wide but stretching a good thirty yards or more back behind the house. Space had not been at a premium when these places had been built.

The rear garden was accessed via a gate, with limited parking behind on a private lane. It was tight and not ideal, but the house hadn't been designed with the needs of the modern car owner in mind. The gate itself was opened using a security code. It was something Hannah had installed after she had moved in, citing Peter's lax security. It had been his house before it was hers and he used to leave the gate unlocked most of the time for convenience.

Kaylee, therefore, did not need to worry about Jess being left alone in the garden temporarily while she prepared her drink. The cup Jess had asked for was a non-spill type designed specifically for toddlers, with a lid and a spout. It had seen better days and the spout was very tarnished where the girl had chewed on it while she had been teething. It needed replacing but she was very attached to it and had rejected the offer of a new one.

Kaylee filled it with water and a dash of squash, then took a saucer and poured in a little tap water for the ladybirds. Then she went back out through the kitchen door which led directly onto the patio.

Everything was as she had left it, except that there was not a trace of Jess. Kaylee was horrified. The garden was open and laid mainly to lawn. There were no bushes, trees, or sheds that she could be hiding behind. The kitchen door was the only way in and out of the house and there was no way she could have got out through the rear gate. Even if she had known the security code, she wasn't tall enough to reach the keypad.

"Jess!" she called out, feeling a sense of blind panic rising within her. How could the girl have gone? She had been in the house less than two minutes.

She looked around the garden, clutching at straws, as she looked for an explanation. She looked at the fences on both sides and the rear. They were both sturdy and firm six-foot-high wooden structures, held in place by posts at regular intervals. There were no gaps or holes anywhere along their length. She couldn't have got out that way.

The only possible way out was the gate so she ran down the garden, repeatedly calling Jess's name louder and in an increasingly panicked state each time. Then she heard tyres on the gravel in the lane beyond. Had someone somehow got in and abducted the girl? It didn't bear thinking about.

She reached the gate, which was secure and locked. She punched the code into the keypad to open it, praying that somehow she would find the girl safe on the other side. As she opened it, she heard a car door slam, just as she called out, "Jess," once more in desperation.

Chapter Four
July 2023

Kaylee's fears intensified when there was no sign of Jess on the other side of the gate. Instead, she was confronted by Hannah, with a distressed look on her face. It was her car door that Kaylee had heard slam and her maternal instincts had kicked in as soon as she had heard the younger woman's anguished calls.

"What's happened?" demanded Hannah. "Where's Jess?"

"I'm so sorry, Hannah," said a truly mortified Kaylee. "I only turned my back for a second."

"That's all it takes!" said Hannah, distraught as the confirmation that something had happened to her daughter sank in.

"But she was safe and secure on the lawn. The gate was locked. I don't understand it."

Again, Hannah did not think to connect what had happened to Jess to what had happened to the others. The overriding fear for her daughter overrode any logical thought. The only thing that mattered was that Jess was missing, and in a brief few seconds, all manner of horrific scenarios went through her mind. Then one of her thoughts led her to make a connection, even though there was no evidence for the conclusion she jumped to.

"Oh my God!" she cried. "Harry Richards!"

"Who is Harry Richards?" asked Kaylee.

"A convicted sex offender we were holding after he exposed himself at the swimming pool yesterday. He's the reason I was called in early this morning. We had him in custody overnight but somehow he escaped. Now Jess has gone missing. He could have taken her!"

"Think for a minute, Hannah," urged Kaylee, desperately trying to get her to think straight. "How could he have got in here? And spirited her away? It's not possible."

Kaylee was distressed herself but was managing to reason things out rather better than Hannah was. Even so, nothing could alter the fact that she had been the one in charge of the girl, and thus couldn't shake off an all-consuming feeling of guilt, whatever the reason for Jess's disappearance.

For Hannah, things had escalated way beyond the level where rational thought came into play, and now her imagination kicked into overdrive.

"My daughter is missing and there is a sexual predator on the loose," she said, breaking down. Tears began to roll down her face and she began to sob uncontrollably. "He's kidnapped her, I know he has."

"Has he done this sort of thing before? I thought you said he was a flasher."

"He is, but he's got convictions for sexual assault too. Against two of his ex-girlfriends and a work colleague."

"But they were all adults?"

"Yes," said Hannah.

"So he has no history of offences against children?"

"Well, no," said Hannah. "But that doesn't mean he isn't capable of it."

"I don't think it can possibly have been him," said Kaylee. "How could he have got past me? Or you, in the lane? There are only two ways in and out of the garden. Through the kitchen, where I was, or through the gate. He could not have got past us so there must be some other explanation. Contact the station and get every officer you've got on the case. Then we'll go and search ourselves, and ask the neighbours if they saw anything. We'll find her, I promise."

"Thank you," said Hannah at Kaylee's comforting words, before tearfully pulling out her phone and calling the station.

While this was going on, Lauren had gone into the town centre out of sheer boredom. Staring at the faded photos on her teenage bedroom walls wasn't her idea of fun. It was depressing. The necessity for her to be there was a reminder of how she needed to get her life back on track, and fast.

After heading downstairs in search of food, she found herself in a heated argument with her mother who confronted her with a demand for rent and food money upfront. She could have just gone back upstairs and started on her mother's huge collection of tins, but the prospect of tinned peaches and tuna didn't get the taste buds tingling.

Frustrated and angry, she stormed out of the house and walked into town with no clear idea of where she was going or why. It was now teatime, and her hunger was still unfulfilled. She decided to go to McDonald's, but upon arrival, she was informed of a lengthy queue due to staff shortages. A flustered teenage girl who was cleaning the tables explained that a couple of team members had failed to turn up for their shift.

She wouldn't be able to afford to eat out like this again if she couldn't find work, not until she got the deposit back on her flat, and that could take weeks. As she ate, she weighed up her options. What sort of job would suit her?

When she had finished her meal, she decided to revisit her old haunt, The Red Lion. She had messaged Kaylee to see if she was up for a drink but hadn't received a response. Undeterred, she decided to venture inside alone. She had no reservations about going in by herself as she was familiar with the locals, having worked some shifts there over the Christmas period a few years ago. It wasn't going to be a long session, though. She didn't have the money.

They were all there when she went in, the usual suspects as she called them. There was Andy, the alcoholic failed musician who spent all day, every day, sitting on the same bar stool downing pint after pint of lager despite having no obvious source of funding. He had been wearing the same faded double denim outfit as long as she had known him. She had a suspicion he never took it off.

He was flanked on the left by a rotund, know-it-all chap who was known as the Beast after a quiz guru on a popular daytime television show. As captain of the pub's quiz team, he had given himself this nomenclature to confirm, in his considered opinion, his vast general knowledge. He thought this gave him an aura of respect, but in truth most of the other people in the pub thought he was a bit of twat.

Perched on a stool to Andy's right was Nobby, a middle-aged man who always appeared overdressed for the pub in his suit and tie. His primary interest was gambling and he was rarely seen without a *Racing Post* tucked under his arm. He liked to think of himself as analytical, methodical and the brains of the pub and had consequently attempted to give himself a nickname too. He had tried to get them to call him the Professor, claiming that was what he had been known as at school. It hadn't really caught on. Self-made nicknames seldom did.

Behind the bar, serving up drinks and dispensing what he believed to be sage advice, was Richard Kent, the pub's proprietor and a former police officer. As Lauren approached the bar, she could hear the familiar sounds of an alcohol-fuelled disagreement taking place – a not uncommon occurrence in this establishment.

"And I can't see why you can't turn over so I can watch the five o'clock at Ascot," protested Nobby.

"Because we want to watch The Ashes," said the Beast, who had his eyes fixed on the large TV sited above the pool table at the end of the room. "It's the final test!"

"Who's we?" asked Nobby. "You mean you, don't you? What's so special about some boring cricket match that goes on for five days until England lose or it ends in a draw? The race at Ascot will take two minutes. It's the last race in the placepot and I'm still in! It could be a big dividend today. Tell him, Andy!"

"What's in it for me?" asked Andy, tipping his almost empty pint glass suggestively in Nobby's direction.

"A pint if my horse makes the frame."

"Can I have it in advance?"

"No."

"Forget it, then. Your bet is bound to go wrong, it always does."

"Thanks very much! I thought we were mates!" He turned to Kent behind the bar and added, "Come on, Richard, just switch over for five minutes."

"Don't listen to him," insisted The Beast. "The Ashes is one of the most important events in the sporting calendar. First contested in 1882, it has been held…"

"Bloody hell it's like having a walking Wikipedia in the pub. Has anyone ever told you how boring you are?" asked Nobby. "Come on, change the channel over for five minutes!

England's already lost the series anyway so what does it matter? Plus they'll probably all be going off for an hour's tea or something soon. Or it'll start raining. You aren't going to miss anything."

Kent looked around the pub, where he could see a couple of tables where the customers were engrossed in the cricket. Although Nobby was one of his best customers, it wasn't worth his while. And the other people weren't regulars. If he upset them, they might not come back and that meant loss of revenue.

"Look here, Nobby, I don't see why you can't just go next door to Coral's and watch the race there."

"I've just got a full pint. Last time I did that, he drank it," he said, gesturing at Andy.

"I'll put it behind the bar, it will be fine," said Kent, just as Lauren made her way up to the bar. "Well, hello, stranger! Back for a visit?"

The others looked across appreciatively. They had enjoyed having Lauren behind the bar during her brief previous spell of employment and Andy had made it obvious that he had a soft spot for her.

"More like back for good," she said. "I've had enough of Oxford. The people there are too up themselves. I miss the raw wit and simplistic banter of you guys back here."

This was said tongue-in-cheek, but they didn't pick up on her thinly veiled insult.

"Nothing simplistic about me, darling," said Andy. "I'm the height of sophistication."

"Really? You keep it well hidden."

"Fine, I'll go to the betting shop, then!" exclaimed Nobby, annoyed at Lauren's entrance interrupting the previous discussion. "But don't expect any favours from me when I collect. I'm looking at over a grand here, at least. I was going to share it with you guys, drinks all round for the rest of the night. And it's my birthday today as well. Not that you lot care."

"That means you've got to get a round in, mate," said Andy. "It's the tradition. How old are you, anyway?"

"Well, if you must know, it's my sixtieth. I was hoping we could all celebrate together."

"Bloody, hell, is that all? I thought you were older than that," said Andy.

"Do you know what? Sod the lot of you. I'll spend my winnings in Ye Olde Chapel instead."

"No, don't do that," said Kent hurriedly, once again thinking about his takings.

"Too late," said Nobby. "Enjoy your boring cricket."

With that he stormed off out of the pub, ignored by the rest of them, which annoyed him even further. They had already turned their attention back to the attractive young woman who had just graced them with her presence. It was a rarity for them these days.

"What are you up to these days?" asked Kent. "Have you got a job back here?"

"No job," said Lauren. "I'm resting, as they say in the acting world."

"That's interesting," said Kent. "Because we're looking for staff here. And if I remember rightly, you worked here briefly before, didn't you? When Craig was the landlord?"

"Yeah, give her a job," interrupted Andy. "I'd much prefer to look at her all night rather than your ugly mug."

"Yes, thank you for your input, Andy. Seriously, Lauren, you could be just what we're looking for."

"I was kind of hoping you might say something like that," said Lauren. "It's one of the reasons I came in here. Another was vodka. After the grief I've had off my mother today, you had better make it a large one."

"I'm going to have to run it by Debs first," said Kent, referring to his long-suffering wife. She ran the pub's restaurant, which was situated in a separate area on the other side of the building.

"Ha! What are you, a man or a mouse?" said Andy. He was now short of conversational companions, following Nobby's departure and the Beast's decision to move along the bar, closer to the television.

"Debs manages all the staffing issues," explained Kent.

"When I had a woman, all the important decisions were down to me," said Andy. "I didn't need to run anything by my missus."

"Yes, and she left you, didn't she?" said Lauren.

"Well, err…"

"I rest my case."

"Speak of the devil," said Andy, as Debs emerged from the door that linked the bar with the restaurant, looking flushed and stressed.

"What is up, my sweet?" asked Kent.

"Janice hasn't shown up. She's meant to be waitressing this evening and was supposed to be here at half past four. It's gone five now and no sign. She's not answering her phone, either."

"Fret not, my dear, I have the perfect solution to your problem. Lauren here is looking for work. Perhaps she can step into the breach."

"I don't know about that," said Lauren. "I was thinking more along the lines of bar work rather than waiting tables."

Debs looked her up and down. She hadn't met Lauren before and thought she looked a little, well, for want of a better word, tarty.

"Got any experience?"

"Oh, loads," said Lauren cheekily. "But possibly not the kind you're referring to."

"Hmmm," said Debs, mulling it over. This brazen young mare would doubtless be an asset to the pub. But did she want her working alongside her husband on a day-to-day basis? Never mind, she could worry about that later. She desperately needed help in the restaurant right now and who else was she going to find at short notice?

"OK," she said, coming to a decision. "You can waitress for me tonight and if you do well, we may be able to talk about something more permanent afterwards – including bar work."

"Perfect," said Lauren, pleased to be back in the saddle already. A job meant money and that meant more independence. The sooner she cut bonds with her mother again, the better.

Next door, in the betting shop, Nobby had arrived just in time to see the horses going into the stalls for the sixth race of the day at Ascot. This was the crucial leg of his placepot, which was a lottery-style bet which involved picking a horse to be placed in the first six races at a meeting. If all six obliged, you won a share of the pot. How much that amounted to depended on the number of winning tickets.

It was rather like the old football pools where the jackpot would vary wildly according to the number of score draws that came up. With the placepot, the more fancied runners that failed to make the frame, the better the dividend would be.

Nobby had successfully navigated his way to this last leg via a series of speculative selections and was now looking at a potentially lucrative pick-up. And from here on it should be plain sailing. He had played safe in this last race and gone for the hot favourite, ridden by the current champion jockey. All it needed to do was finish in the first three, and he would pick up what, by his reckoning, would be a four-figure sum. And that lot at the pub weren't getting their hands on a penny of it.

It would have been nice if there had been a crowd in the shop to cheer on his selection with him but sadly the days of camaraderie and banter in busy betting shops were long gone. Other than a couple of addicts playing the roulette machines, the shop was empty. Nobby wondered why the big betting companies bothered keeping these shops open at all. He, like nearly all punters nowadays, placed all his bets online.

The race went beautifully, to begin with. It was all he could have hoped for. The jockey kept the favourite just off the pace and on the outside, avoiding the risk of getting boxed in on the rails. As they approached the final furlong he cruised up to the front, going easily, and began to pull clear. Never mind being in the first three, he was going to win, and win easily.

Then something unprecedented happened. Deep inside the closing stages, the horse simply vanished from beneath the jockey who suddenly found himself hurtling through the air and crashing down to the turf. Jockeys were tough cookies who knew how to protect themselves in a fall and the champion's instincts quickly kicked in, but it still hurt like hell as he hit the ground. His worries were not over, either, as there was the danger of being trampled by another runner. Fortunately, he was so far clear, the other jockeys had ample time to take avoiding action.

Nobby let out a groan. He wasn't concerned about the welfare of the jockey, or the impossibility of what he had just witnessed. A horse, a living, breathing creature had just disappeared into thin air, live on television. The only thing he was feeling was the sickening realisation that his bet had gone down. He couldn't believe the sheer injustice of it all. Every time he seemed to be on the brink of a big win, something came along to scupper it. That on this occasion it was something almost supernatural was irrelevant. He had been stitched up – again.

The two guys playing the machines hadn't even looked up, despite the hysterics of the race commentator, who was going on about how in fifty years of following racing he had never seen anything like it. However, the rest of the world was soon going ballistic. Within minutes, the clip was all over social media and Mystic Mick and others of his ilk were falling over each over to be the first to get their theories about what they had just seen up on YouTube.

Back in London, Dominic Campbell was watching the playback of the race with dismay. It was going to be very difficult to cover this up. He was going to need every tool at his disposal to come up with an even halfway plausible explanation for the public. There was only one thing for it. He was going to have to insist that the Prime Minister call an emergency COBR meeting.

The leader was spending the weekend at Chequers, his country retreat, so Dominic used a number that was reserved only for times of extreme threat to the nation. It was guaranteed to activate the PM's phone, even if it was silent or switched off, overriding all protocols, and issuing a piercing alarm. He simply couldn't fail to pick it up. It had only been used once before when the conflict had broken out in Ukraine, and he remembered the previous Prime Minister at the time complaining that it had almost deafened him.

But today, that wasn't going to happen. Because when Dominic dialled the number, all he got in return was a recorded message telling him that it had not been possible to connect the call. That wasn't possible unless the phone had been deactivated or destroyed.

Concerned, he rang the PM's wife, knowing that they were spending the weekend together. She answered right away, giving him more news that he did not want to hear.

It seemed that the Prime Minister had vanished.

Chapter Five
July 2023

Despite the best attempts of Charlie and Kaylee to pacify Hannah, she remained inconsolable. Her child was missing and the anguish she felt was overwhelming all other considerations. The unprecedented nature of the situation made it even more unbearable. She was used to being able to come up with rational explanations for things, and the inability to find one to fit this scenario had left her feeling so nauseous that she wasn't far off being physically sick from the worry.

By nightfall, several hours had passed since Jess had gone missing and there was still no trace of her anywhere. Despite a thorough search by every police officer Hannah could lay her hands on, things seemed increasingly hopeless. The intervening hours had also done nothing to assuage Kaylee's feelings of guilt. She had contacted Charlie, who had just returned to town after his night out with Josh, and he rushed over to Hannah's house to help. Realistically though, moral support was all he could offer.

Now, seated in the living room, they were analysing the situation as well as trying to provide reassurance to Hannah. But their arguments were having little impact.

"But she can't just have vanished by herself! Someone must have taken her," said Hannah, which was the conclusion she kept coming back to.

"Just think about it, Hannah," urged Charlie. "The gate was locked. There was no evidence anyone came in or out. Your officers have been over everything with a fine-tooth comb."

"That's easy for you to say, but what I am expected to think when there's a convicted sex offender on the loose? You two aren't parents. You couldn't possibly understand what I'm going through."

"Maybe not, but perhaps that's just as well. We can look at the situation objectively."

"Don't preach to me about objectivity and subjectivity," said Hannah. "My daughter is missing. How do you expect me to look at it?"

"Look at everything else that has been going on. She's not the only missing person," said Kaylee. "You admitted yourself that it was highly improbable that Harry Richards could have escaped from the police station."

"Then there was that trucker that went missing," added Charlie. "Another unexplained disappearance. Yet, despite the media being all over it yesterday, it's as if it never happened today. Look at this."

He took his phone out of his pocket and pulled up the BBC's website. The news headline was something about a record-breaking heatwave and forest fires in Rhodes. There was also something about rising mortgage rates and the cost-of-living crisis plus an update on The Ashes. But missing persons? Nothing.

"See?" he said. "If you turn on the television, it will be the same."

Hannah thought about the cancelled press conference and her call with Dan Bradley, just before Jess had gone missing. Even in her addled state of mind, she could not deny that there was something out of the ordinary going on.

"Blimey, look at this," said Charlie, who had pulled up a link to a video that Josh had just sent him on his phone. It was a clip of the mysterious disappearing horse that had ended Nobby's placepot dreams.

He showed it to Hannah and Kaylee.

"That could easily have been faked," said Hannah.

"It's difficult to tell on such a small screen. Let's look on the television," suggested Kaylee.

Hannah had a smart TV so they logged into YouTube and looked up the clip. But they couldn't find it.

"Where is it?" asked Kaylee. "Charlie, what's the address of it on your phone?"

"I can't find it either," said Charlie, clicking back on the link that Josh had sent him. "It says that this video is no longer available."

"They've pulled it," said Kaylee. "You see, something is going on that they don't want us to see."

"And who are they exactly?" asked Hannah.

"People in power who want to keep the public in the dark about what is going on," said Charlie. "And it's obvious something big is happening. Now I know that's not going to be of any comfort to you under the present circumstances but surely you must be able to see how strange all of this."

"OK, I can," admitted Hannah, who could no longer ignore the mounting evidence. "But none of that changes the fact that my daughter is missing. No matter how impossible the situation, she's lost somewhere, possibly alone, and probably very frightened."

"You know, I've been giving this a lot of thought," said Charlie, "and perhaps everything that is happening is not quite as unprecedented as we might think."

"People vanishing into thin air?" asked Kaylee. "It's not something I've ever seen before, outside of a science fiction movie."

"But you have," said Charlie. "It happened to you, remember? Think back to everything that happened with the time bubble when we first discovered it. You disappeared and it took you two days into the future. Peter's travelling through it into the future right now. When you went through it, there was a massive missing person operation, just like there is now with Jess. You must be able to see the parallels."

"Yes, but this can't be down to the time bubble. That is in a fixed place in a tunnel. It doesn't move. And it can only take one person at a time so with Peter inside, it's harmless right now."

61

"As far as we know," said Charlie. "Perhaps something has changed."

"Are you suggesting that somehow it's become mobile and it's gobbling people up?" asked Kaylee.

"No, not necessarily. But what if there are more time bubbles that we don't know about? Perhaps all the people who have gone missing have fallen into them. It's worth exploring the possibility, don't you think? I'm going to give Josh a call. I think it's time we got the old team back together to investigate."

"If Charlie is right, and Jess is in a time bubble, then she'll reappear at some point. That must give you some hope, Hannah."

"I want to believe that it is that simple," she replied. "But let's be honest, it is only a theory Charlie has come up with. That's all."

"You must not give up hope, Hannah," said Kaylee. "It may be only a theory, but it's a plausible one."

"I guess so. Listen, could you both stay here tonight? I don't want to be here on my own."

"Of course," said Kaylee. "It's the least we can do."

The following morning, two important meetings took place. In London, a rare Sunday morning emergency COBR meeting had been called to discuss the situation.

And at Hannah's house, she, Charlie, and Kaylee had been joined by Josh and Lauren.

"I do hope this is something important, dragging me out of bed at half past nine on a Sunday morning," said Lauren, as she stood bleary-eyed on the doorstep. It had been a very late night for her. The waitressing had gone well, and after the restaurant closed she had stayed on with the regulars for a few drinks that had continued well into the small hours. A large chunk of the money she had earned had gone on vodka.

When she returned home, her mother was still up and started excitedly badgering her with more conspiracy theories about missing persons. Lauren, in her inebriated state, had rebuffed her, leading to another pointless argument. However, as she was about to find out, perhaps her mother hadn't been so far off the mark after all.

"Oh, it's important," said Josh, who had answered the door. "And be careful what you say. Please don't start banging on about how much vodka you had last night and who you shagged. Hannah is in a very fragile state right now."

"I didn't shag anyone last night. You sound like my mother. What do you take me for?"

"Do you really want me to answer that?" said Josh.

"You know, if I didn't know better, I might have detected a hint of jealousy there," she replied. "Feeling regretful, are we, thinking about what you've been missing out on since you dumped me?"

"If I recall, we parted ways by mutual consent," said Josh. "You're not cut out for long-term relationships and you know it."

"Nor were you, the last time I checked. I can't envisage you being all loved up with anyone in the way Charlie and Kaylee are. You're just as bad as me and you know it. Otherwise, you'd have settled down with some nerdy academic type from university by now."

"If you say so," said Josh, leading her through the hallway and opening the kitchen door where the others were waiting.

"Morning, all!" said Lauren, appreciating the welcome aroma coming from the bubbling pot on the side. "I'm glad to see you've got some coffee on. I'm going to need it."

The others were already busy consuming copious amounts of caffeine, and Lauren was pleased to also see a plate of croissants on the table. They were a delicacy that she always enjoyed. What she wasn't so happy to see was the shocking state that Hannah was in. Normally, she was so calm, confident, and well presented but this morning was the complete opposite.

She hadn't bothered to get dressed and was still in her night attire of an old t-shirt covered by a dressing gown. She had dark circles under her eyes and the surrounding skin was puffy and swollen. The eyes themselves were red and bloodshot and it was clear she had been crying – a lot. Her creased brow merely added to the general appearance of worry and stress as she sat leaning forward onto the kitchen table, with her head in her left hand and a cup of coffee in the other.

"Do you have to be so jovial?" said Charlie. "Bearing in mind what's happened."

"Sorry," said Lauren, realising her faux pas. "I take it there's no news then?"

"None," said Charlie.

"I barely slept a wink all night," said Hannah, looking up. "I just can't get the thoughts of all the things that could have happened to her out of my head."

"That's why we're all here," said Josh. "I know how difficult this is for you, Hannah, but this is no ordinary missing person case. Something bigger is happening that we don't yet understand but we are going to try and figure it out. If we can do that, then we can try and find Jess."

"He's right," said Charlie. "Like I said last night, people are disappearing all over the place. Social media is awash with stories, even if the mainstream media are pretending nothing's happening."

"So where are they going?" asked Lauren.

"Or when," said Josh. "None of the missing people has turned up, as far as we know. My number one theory is that they've travelled forwards in time. Like we did, before, in the time bubble."

"OK, so even if it's a case of when rather than where, that still doesn't tell us why," said Charlie. "Is this happening by accident, at random, or is it by design? And if it is by design, who is orchestrating it and for what purpose?"

"That's what we've got to work out," said Josh. "But all those people have to be going somewhere."

"There's this guy on YouTube that my mum watches who had a video about this yesterday," said Lauren. "His name is Mystic Mick."

Charlie groaned and said, "Oh, not that nutter. He's a grade-one conspiracy theorist. YouTube is full of them."

"Oh, I agree. But my mum is convinced that he is bang on the money with this one," said Lauren.

"And when have you ever taken any notice of anything she says?" said Kaylee. "You've ranted on countless times about how much you can't stand her."

"Well, that's true," admitted Lauren. "But perhaps we ought to look at what some of these people are saying. There may be hundreds of wacky ideas out there about what's going on, but one of these crackpots might just get lucky and hit on the answer. Or at least say something to put us on the right track."

"It won't do any harm to check a few of them out, I suppose," said Josh.

"Well I think it's a waste of time," said Kaylee. "These people are only interested in getting hits for their channel."

"If we can even find anything," added Charlie. "That footage of the horse race vanished nearly as quickly as the horse itself."

They went through to the living room, put on the television again and scoured it for videos on the subject. It was surprisingly difficult, with censorship seemingly in full flow. Mystic Mick's channel seemed to have vanished completely.

"I think we'll be better off scouring social media," said Charlie. "There was plenty of stuff trending about this on Twitter earlier. Perhaps we should trawl through some of it, see if we can come up with anything before they remove it all."

"They can't censor everything people post, surely?" asked Lauren.

"Oh, they'll try," said Josh. "So we had better get started."

The disappearances were indeed the talk of the internet, and it seemed every man, woman and their dogs had a theory. But most of them were completely outlandish.

"One guy here reckons that we are all being transported to Mars," said Josh, flicking through Twitter on his phone.

"I found one that claims that the Russians have invented a device that can vaporise people at a distance and is culling us one by one so they can take over the world," said Charlie.

"Great," said Hannah sarcastically. "These guys are really going to help me get my daughter back, aren't they?"

"I told you it was all nonsense," said Kaylee.

"Listen to this one," said Josh. "It's all down to a shadowy secret world government who are preparing to take over by getting rid of everyone they identify as a political dissident."

"And these political dissidents include innocent three-year-old girls, do they?" said Kaylee. "Face it, this is all speculative fantasy from sad cases sitting in their bedrooms with nothing better to do. I don't think anyone knows what's going on. Including the government."

"I think you are probably right," said Josh.

He was right. In London, Dominic had summoned as many ministers as he could get hold of to the emergency meeting as well as a few senior government advisors. They were desperately trying to make sense of what was going on – and failing miserably.

"Is the media blackout still holding?" he asked the Minister for Culture, Media and Sport.

"Yes," came the reply from the young man in his mid-thirties, who had only been recently appointed. "But people aren't stupid. They know something is going on. You need only look at Twitter to see that."

"Shut it down, then," suggested the lady immediately to Dominic's right. Sporting a brunette shoulder-length hairstyle, she was smartly dressed in a tailored navy suit, and leaning forward in a pose that exuded confidence. Her name was Jenna

Rose and she held the post of Foreign Secretary. During her climb up the political ladder, she had acquired a reputation for being ruthless and had trodden on plenty of toes along the way. Perhaps too many, because only weeks previously she had lost a leadership election she had been convinced she would win. But at the last moment, the party membership hadn't voted the way she had expected.

The incoming Prime Minister, David Choi, had been very gracious in victory, giving Jenna a senior ministerial role, which he hadn't needed to do. However she was bitter and resentful, and ever since the defeat had been trying to think of ways to stab him in the back and claim the throne that she considered rightfully hers.

"If we do that, Jenna, it will only look even more suspicious," said Dominic. "And then what do you think will happen?"

"Look, you cannot cover up what is going on, Dominic," said Simon Grant, the Chancellor of the Exchequer. "I know that's your modus operandi, but people are vanishing all over the country, right in front of other people's eyes. If we ignore that, we're risking losing control. It's far better we go out there and assure people we are on top of the situation."

"Are you suggesting a press conference?" said Jenna. "Like we did for the pandemic?"

"Yes," said Simon. "The cat is already out of the bag and we need to explain that we know what is happening and we are putting plans in place to deal with it."

"What do you suggest we tell them when we don't know ourselves what is going on?" said Dominic. "And who is going to speak to them? People will expect the Prime Minister. How are we going to explain his absence?" He was feeling increasingly exasperated by the situation. He was used to being in control and right now he was most certainly not.

"I'll do it," said Jenna, sensing an opportunity.

"Leaping straight into the dead man's shoes, I see," said Dominic. "I expected nothing less of you."

"We don't know he's dead and someone's got to take charge," she replied. "Otherwise we're going to have anarchy."

"I quite agree," said Simon. "I'm not sure you are the most appropriate person, though. I mean, you just lost a leadership vote."

"I came second," she said. "And where did you come, precisely? Fifth, wasn't it? I rest my case. Now let's get on with thinking about what I'm going to say. Do we have any hard facts on how many people are missing?"

"I got some bods at Imperial College to run some modelling," said Dominic. "And it's not good news. Since Friday, when this all started, it's estimated that at least 5% of the population has disappeared. And it's not just people. There are reports of animals going missing too."

"And this is still continuing?" asked Jenna.

"It is," said Dominic.

"Then the implications are huge. Look at what happened on the M40 and then imagine what would happen if say, a pilot, disappeared."

"That's why we have always had two pilots on every flight," said Dominic. "In case one gets taken ill."

"It's still way too risky," continued Jenna. "We should ground all air travel immediately. In fact, make that all travel. Let's close the borders and declare a lockdown. For everyone's safety."

"How are you going to justify that?" asked Simon. "It's not like there is a killer virus roaming loose, is it?"

As so often seemed to be the case, he and Jenna were at loggerheads. She was authoritarian and he was libertarian, which meant they were instinctively opposed on these sorts of issues.

"We scare the hell out of them," piped up a lady at the end of the table who had remained silent until this point. Her name was Suzanne Michaelson, and she was the head of the government's psychological unit. This department had been set up to monitor, and if necessary control, public behaviour in times of crisis.

"How?" said Simon.

"Convince them there is a tangible threat. You've seen all the rumours circulating on the internet. Make them think there is some foreign power with a weapon that can zap you if you set foot outside the house. Or that it's aliens."

"No one is going to believe that in a million years," said Simon.

"Oh, you would be surprised what you can make people believe if you present it in the right way," said Suzanne.

"And what's that going to achieve, exactly? The country will grind to a halt. How are people going to get food? How is the food even going to get delivered to the supermarkets?"

"It's not my job to figure that out, Simon," said Suzanne. "I can only make recommendations. You're the ones making the decisions."

"If things carry on like this, we won't need any food," said Dominic, trying to wrest back control of the conversation. "Because there will be nobody left to eat it. The guys at Imperial modelled a worst-case scenario that at the current rate, there will be nobody left on Earth by the autumn."

"They've been wrong before," said Simon. "Frequently."

"It doesn't matter whether they are right or wrong," said Jenna. "We are in charge and it is our responsibility. We need to do what is right to protect the people, no matter what the cost."

"I don't like the sound of that," said Simon. "It sounds a bit like the end justifying the means to me."

"It doesn't matter, ultimately, whether you like the sound of it or not," said Jenna. "If what Dominic says here is true, we're all living on borrowed time anyway. The longer we maintain the illusion of normality, the better. I don't know what you want to do, but I don't plan to spend my last days fighting over the last tin of beans in Tesco, do you?"

"No," admitted Simon.

"Good. You agree then. I'll take charge and I'll decide what is to be done."

Sometimes she could hardly believe her audacity, but nobody challenged her. The bossy demeanour which had worked so well in elevating her to her current position had come up trumps again. The great thing about the current crisis was that her rivals had no counterargument because they were just as much in the dark as she was.

Elsewhere, the theories were coming thick and fast. It didn't matter how much social media was censored, nothing could stop good old-fashioned word of mouth, short of sealing the entire population in their homes.

Josh, Charlie, and Lauren were making their way into town, leaving Kaylee to take care of Hannah. Lauren was heading back to the pub, where she had agreed to do a lunchtime session behind the bar. Charlie and Josh had decided to go down to the tunnel where the time bubble was situated, just to check there wasn't anything unusual going on. They considered it unlikely, but it needed ruling out, nonetheless.

When the three of them got into town, there was a strange atmosphere. There were not as many people around as usual, and there was a palpable sense of unease in the air. It wasn't something Lauren could put her finger on, but something didn't feel right.

As they walked down the street, their attention was caught by a small gathering that had formed up ahead. Intrigued, they made their way closer and soon noticed a man standing on an old beer crate addressing a group of around twenty people at the top of his voice.

"It's Bob the bible basher," said Josh, recognising the middle-aged man on the box. He had been practically a standing fixture in the town the whole time they had been growing up. Every weekend he stood in the pedestrianised street, urging everyone who passed to devote their lives to Jesus. Usually, nobody took any notice of him. Until today.

"The moment has come! The time of Revelation is upon us. It is time to repent and believe in our Saviour, Jesus Christ, his Father, God, and the Holy Ghost. Those who do will ascend to sit by his side. The process has already begun!"

The small crowd, desperate for something to believe in, were hanging on to his every word. Bob, which was probably not his real name, just the nickname he had acquired, was in his element. After all these years of being ignored, it seemed he was finally getting the attention he craved.

"The righteous and the holy have already joined him. They have gone to the Rapture, and it is not too late for you to join them. But do not delay. Hurry, and repent, while you still have time. Otherwise, when judgement is passed, you will burn with all the other sinners as this world is consumed in a fiery hell!"

"The Rapture?" asked Lauren, who had little interest in religious matters. "What's that?"

"Some Christians believe that on Judgement Day, when the world ends, all true believers will rise to the clouds and join God in heaven. They call this process the Rapture," said Charlie.

"And this is Bob's explanation for what's happening?"

"It's no more unlikely than anything else we've heard," said Josh. "And this lot certainly seem to believe it."

"That's because they are desperate to rationalise the situation," said Charlie. "Why do you think all these theories are proliferating on the internet? It's a basic human trait to need to understand the world. So we come up with explanations. Sometimes they are scientific and based on fact, in other cases, based on religion, superstition or imagination."

"Bob's theory doesn't work, though, does it?" said Josh. "I mean, look at that sex offender that vanished, the one Hannah told us about. He doesn't sound like the sort of person to be welcome at the Pearly Gates, does he?"

"Maybe not," said Charlie. "But this crowd gathered around Bob seem to be lapping up his every word."

"Because they need something to believe in," said Kaylee. "He is telling them what they want to hear."

"Fascinating," said Josh. "They never took a blind bit of notice of him before."

They watched fascinated as Bob continued to preach to the steadily growing crowd.

"Do not wait any longer! Join those of us who truly believe here today and we shall all ascend to the Rapture together!"

Chapter Six
July 2023

"I must now give you one simple instruction," said Jenna Rose, echoing words spoken by another prime minister a few years previously. She paused for dramatic effect, fixing her unblinking eyes on the camera with a steely gaze, and added, "You must stay at home."

It was 8 o'clock on Sunday evening and all television audience records had just been broken as Jenna broadcast the government's explanation of the nature of the threat facing the world to over thirty million viewers. To highlight just how serious the situation was, she also took the opportunity to break the news that the Prime Minister was missing and she was assuming control.

Her words had been chosen carefully with the help of Suzanne and her team of psychologists. She felt she had delivered them with aplomb, leaving the watching millions in no doubt that if they disobeyed her instructions they would be risking their lives.

Similar broadcasts were going out across the globe, conveying the same message that had been hastily agreed on by the majority of the world's leaders.

In the Watson household, Patricia was lapping up every word. As soon as Jenna finished speaking she turned to her daughter to crow.

"You see! Mystic Mick was right! It is an alien invasion."

"Aliens? Really?" said an exasperated Lauren. "You don't seriously believe all this nonsense, do you?"

"How else do you explain it? They're beaming us all up to their ships like they do on *Star Trek*."

"And staying inside is going to protect us, is it? I find it hard to believe that an alien race with the technology to spirit people away in an energy beam can't reach you if you are indoors. And what about when we are allowed out for our one trip a day to go food shopping? Are we safe then?"

"You heard what Jenna Rose said. Provided you wear a hat, you'll be fine. It's not like I need that much food anyway. Only fresh stuff and even if I can't get that, I'll be OK. I've been preparing for this day for a long time."

"So that's what all that food in my bedroom is for?"

"Yes, Mystic Mick warned us something big was coming and that we needed to prepare. All you sheep didn't take any notice, but who's laughing now? I've got enough here to survive for years."

"Honestly, Mum, I don't know where to start with you sometimes. This is all bull excrement of the highest order. Mystic Mick is a grifter and Jenna Rose is talking out of her arse. I'm going out."

"You can't go out! It's against the law."

"And who is going to stop me, exactly? You? Perhaps I'm not quite the sheep you think I am!"

Similar arguments were taking place all over the country. On a quiet night in The Red Lion, where Andy was one of the few remaining customers, he was stating his case to be allowed to carry on drinking.

"You heard what the acting Prime Minister said. Everyone is to go home immediately," said Debs, who was standing next to Kent behind the bar.

"She didn't say you had to go home, she said you had to stay at home. And that it wasn't safe to go out without a hat. Well, I haven't got a hat, so if you send me outside, you could be sending me to my death. Is that something you want on your conscience?"

"You can borrow one of Richard's. He's got a couple of old baseball caps knocking about somewhere upstairs."

"Really?" said Andy, turning to Kent incredulously. "Somehow I can't imagine you in a baseball cap. An old man's flat cap is more your image."

Kent was horrified at the thought of having to shut the pub. The financial implications didn't bear thinking about, especially right in the middle of summer during the first few days of decent weather for weeks. Therefore, for once he came to Andy's defence, despite the insult regarding his choice of headwear.

"You know, this is all a bit sudden, my love," said Kent. "We can't afford to shut the pub again. Remember what happened last time? Pouring all that beer down the drain was one of the most traumatic experiences of my whole life. There's no need for Andy to rush off. At least let him stay here until he's spent all his money, sorry, I mean until it's dark. Maybe he'll be safer going home then."

"Yeah, the aliens won't be able to spot me under cover of darkness!" said Andy. "Nice thinking, guvnor!"

The only other remaining customers, a young couple who had been playing pool when the announcement had come through on the television, finished their drinks and left. Now, only Andy remained.

"I think I'll join you in that pint," said Kent. "The more we drink the less we waste."

"That's the spirit!" said Andy appreciatively. "Let's have a few more beers while we wait for the aliens to come and zap us, eh? It's not like we've got anything better to do!"

"One more pint, and then he's got to go, Richard," said Debs, giving him a look which he knew not to mess with. "I mean it!"

While they got on with their drinking, back at Hannah's she had been watching the announcement along with Josh, Kaylee, and Charlie. Now they were discussing the implications.

"So, the official story now is that my daughter's been abducted by aliens?" said Hannah. "I can't believe they've got

80

the audacity to come out with this stuff. And, presumably, they expect me to police the lockdown?"

"That's all it is, a story. I'm convinced they haven't got a clue what's going on," said Josh. "This isn't like during the pandemic when people could at least see there was a tangible threat. To conjure up a story about aliens out of thin air is ludicrous."

"So why do it?" asked Kaylee.

"Because they're afraid of society breaking down and they feel they must do something to keep control of the situation," said Josh. "That's why Jenna said that stuff about not panic buying. They are clearly worried about potential food shortages."

"That's the worst thing she could have said," replied Kaylee. "What's the one thing that always happens when people are warned not to panic buy? They rush out to stock up, therefore triggering the very shortages that they are supposedly trying to avoid."

"Like last time with the coronavirus," said Charlie. "The media whipped up a storm and suddenly everyone was fighting over toilet rolls and stuff."

"My dad had about five hundred toilet rolls stacked up in his garage back then," said Josh. "I think he's still using them up now."

"So panic buying is inevitable again, then?" asked Charlie.

"Without a doubt," said Josh. "They've planted the idea in people's minds now. It's just as well that it's Sunday evening and the shops are all shut. If I were you, I would get down to Tesco or Sainsbury as soon as they open tomorrow morning and stock up on whatever you can lay your hands on."

"Won't we just be making the problem worse?" asked Kaylee. "Because that's what everyone is going to do."

"Oh, this is going to get worse. A lot worse. Think about where we are. Right now, we've had a handful of people go missing. But what happens if this keeps up? How many people do you need to keep the world turning? 90%? 70%? What happens when there aren't enough people left to produce food? Or to deliver it to the stores?"

"Chaos," said Charlie, envisaging some distinctly unpleasant scenarios.

"That's why we need to find a solution," said Josh.

"How did you get on with the time bubble this afternoon?" asked Kaylee. "Did you find anything?"

"Nothing, I'm afraid. Charlie and I checked the tunnel over thoroughly and drew a blank. So, I'm going back to Oxford first thing tomorrow morning to talk to Professor Hamilton. We'll put our heads together in the lab and see what we can come up with."

"None of this is going to bring Jess back, though, is it?" said Hannah, who hadn't said much during the past few minutes. She was still very distant and withdrawn.

"It might," said Josh. "Please don't give up hope for her. I'm convinced that all the missing people are safe and sound somewhere. We will do everything we can to find them, I promise."

"Will you be able to get back to Oxford?" said Charlie. "I mean, will the police let people travel?"

"I am the police, remember?" said Hannah. "And I've not been told anything to that effect."

"Perhaps they're leaving you alone, you know, bearing in mind what's happened with Jess," said Kaylee awkwardly. She felt as if she were treading on eggshells just mentioning the girl.

"Maybe," said Hannah. "I will call the station and see if they have been issued with any instructions. But quite honestly, we wouldn't have the resources to stop people if they chose to ignore the lockdown. I guess the government are just banking on people complying with their edicts. I don't see what else they can do unless they're planning on bringing the army in and declaring martial law, which seems a bit drastic."

"Are you sure you feel up to it?" said Kaylee. "Perhaps you ought to be resting."

"No, I don't feel up to it," said Hannah. "But I know that moping about here isn't going to change anything and I want to know what's going on. If we're going to get to the bottom of this then we need all hands to the pump. Including mine."

She spoke to Sergeant Smith, who was manning the station, and then to Dan Bradley in Oxford. They were completely in the dark about what the police were supposed to do. There were existing plans in place for dealing with national emergencies which covered things like wars, viruses, and natural disasters. But there were no guidelines for multiple unexplained disappearances or alien invasions. Those were not scenarios that had been considered feasible when the guidelines had been drawn up. So nobody had a clue what to do.

Neither Hannah nor Dan were fans of Jenna and concluded that her authoritative speech amounted to little more than an ambitious power grab, using aliens as the excuse.

Josh was staying at his family home, currently empty, as his parents were away for a couple of weeks on a road trip to Cornwall. He headed home while Charlie returned to his mother who had called as she was worried about him following the announcement. Kaylee stayed behind with Hannah again, still concerned about her state of mind. But in the morning, it was a problem no longer because by then, her friend was gone.

When Hannah hadn't surfaced, Kaylee took her a cup of coffee, but the room was empty. The bed was ruffled and slept in, but of its occupant there was no sign. She checked the house, and all the doors were still locked, with Hannah's keys hanging up on a hook in the hallway. A further check revealed her car was still in the lane behind the house.

All the signs pointed to the likelihood that Hannah had fallen victim to whatever phenomenon had spirited away the others. So much for people being safe in their homes. They had been right to doubt the previous evening's announcement, but she took no pleasure in concluding that the government was indeed lying. Inside, she felt a growing sense of fear. How much longer would it be until it was her turn? And what would be the nature of whatever fate was to befall her?

In Hannah's case, although Kaylee was understandably concerned, there was also an element of relief. She had hated seeing her friend tormented by the loss of her daughter. At least now her suffering was over. Kaylee tried to remain optimistic and pictured the two of them, wherever they might be, enjoying a tearful and happy reunion. She could only hope that when her time came, she would find them both again.

She had promised to go out and get some provisions, but there seemed little point in doing that now. She might as well go home to Charlie. Then she remembered that he had said something about going out early to beat the rush. She called him, to hear that he was sitting in a traffic queue trying to get into Sainsbury's car park.

"It's bloody ridiculous, this," said Charlie as the driver of a car further behind him in the queue began beeping his horn repeatedly. "The whole damn country has gone out panic buying."

His ageing red Mini, which had seen him through his college days, was starting to get a little overheated. Although it was still early, it looked as if it was going to be another warm day and the sun was already baking down on the roof, radiating waves of heat into the car. He rolled down the window, feeling exasperated at the idiocy of the other drivers for causing this jam. That just by being there he was part of the problem was a point that escaped him. It was a fallacy that befell every driver who had ever been caught in a traffic jam. Their reason for being there was vital, whereas that of all the other drivers was trivial.

"I'll walk down and join you," said Kaylee.

"You'll probably get there before me, the way this traffic's backing up."

Lauren and Patricia were also in the queue, about a hundred yards ahead of Charlie. It had taken them over half an hour to reach the circular ramp that led up to the car park above the store. It took them a further ten minutes to find a parking space on the top deck after which they embarked on a hunt for a trolley. These proved to be remarkably elusive. In the end, they followed someone else back to their car who had filled theirs to the brim. Once they had emptied it, they gave them a pound coin and Lauren took hold of it.

Once it was in her possession she couldn't resist commenting, having watched the woman unload massive amounts of soft drinks, bread rolls, wine, and all manner of other things.

"Having a party?" she asked but got just a blank stare in return. Before she could say more, Patricia began berating her for her lack of headwear.

"Put something on your head, for Christ's sake. Do you want to be spirited away by the aliens?"

"Don't be ridiculous, Mum. Even if that story were true, which it isn't, do you honestly think that old bobble hat you tried to foist on me is going to be strong enough to protect me from the technology these little green men have got?"

"You could have a point there," said Patricia, taking what Lauren was saying at face value, and running her hand across her red woollen hat. "Do you think I should have gone for something stronger? A bicycle helmet, maybe?"

"Why not go the whole hog and mock up something like that guy over there?" suggested Lauren, pointing out a chunky young chap on the other side of the car park who was conspicuous by the shiny bright tinfoil head-covering he had fashioned for himself.

"Yes, that's the stuff. To deflect the rays."

"You seriously believe all this stuff, don't you?"

"You heard what they said on the television," insisted Patricia.

"Yes, and that's another thing. How many times have you told me never to listen to the news? You've been telling me that it is all lies and that I should never pay attention to the mainstream media for years. Now you're doing exactly what they are telling you to do, just like all these other idiots."

As she spoke, she cast her eye around, exasperated to see that most people in the car park were donning headgear of one type or another.

"Better safe than sorry. You'll regret it when the aliens take you away. Though, I expect you're hoping they'll take me first, aren't you? Then you can get your hands on the house. That is what you came back from Oxford for, after all, isn't it? You don't care about me at all, only your inheritance."

"Believe me, I wouldn't be staying with you unless I had no other option. Spirited away or not, I'll be out of your hair as soon as I possibly can."

"Suits me," replied Patricia as they walked through the glass doors on the top deck of the car park that led to the lifts.

"I don't know why you felt the need to come here anyway," said Lauren "You've filled the house with food for precisely this situation. Yet here you are, still trying to get more."

"You can never be over-prepared," was the reply, after which Lauren gave up. It was pointless trying to reason with her.

Everyone that came out of the lift when it arrived, after an age, was loaded up with enough food to feed an army. It did not bode well and when the lift doors opened at ground level they were greeted by a scene of absolute mayhem.

Lauren had never seen so many people inside a supermarket before, not even on Christmas Eve. It was quite literally rammed. Every till was open, and each had lengthy and impatient queues building up. Meanwhile, out on the shop floor, tempers were becoming frayed.

The shoppers were stripping the shelves like locusts on a field of wheat and any semblance of normal etiquette had been abandoned. Lauren watched as some more able-bodied types aggressively barged the older and frailer out of the way, muscling their way to the rapidly dwindling supplies.

She watched, disgusted, as two men wearing motorcycle helmets at the end of one aisle, bundled an elderly lady out of the way. Then they began loading their trolley with every tin of tuna that was left on the shelf, denying the senior citizen the chance to get even one. Incensed, she decided to confront them.

"Wait here," she said to her mum, passing their trolley to her. It would slow her down if she kept hold of it. Unencumbered, she nimbly nipped her way through the crowd and reached the men just as they were loading the last multipack into their trolley.

"What the hell do you think you are doing?" she said. "Put that lot back, right now!"

"Oh, look who it is," said the larger of the two men. "The biggest slag in town. What are you going to do, make me?"

It was only when he spoke that she recognised him from his voice. It was her nemesis from school, Daniel Fisher, and his long-term sidekick, Ryan.

"Believe me, I will," said Lauren. "Look at the state of you. You were a bully at school and now you're bullying old ladies. How old are you, dear?" she added, turning to the lady.

"I'm eighty-nine!" said the sprightly pensioner. "And let me tell you, I've never seen such disgusting behaviour. Not even during the war."

"There you go, Daniel, you should be ashamed of yourself. Now give this lady one of those multipacks."

"Sure, what difference does one pack of four tins make?" he replied. "We've got another eighty in here. Here you go, Gran. Eat them up quickly, though. Hardly worth storing them at your age, is it?"

He handed over four tins, humouring Lauren in the hope that the stupid cow would go away.

"There, satisfied?"

"No, I'm not. Now put back the rest."

"Go fuck yourself."

"I mean it," said Lauren, putting on her meanest face, as a small crowd began to gather. It wasn't the first altercation in the store today, and it wouldn't be the last, but her gutsy outburst had drawn some silent appreciation from the other shoppers.

"Make me," said Dan, trying to tough it out, but Lauren knew he was nowhere near as brave as her. She had outfoxed him several times in the past, and today would be no different.

Without warning, she reached forward and grabbed him by the balls. It wasn't difficult through the flimsy Bermuda shorts he was wearing.

He gasped in shock, as she got a good grip and slowly began to apply pressure to his testicles.

"Now be a good boy, and tell Ryan here to put that tuna back. Otherwise, you'll never get the chance to use these again. That is if you even have before, other than by yourself. And that's a big if."

"Do as she says," he said, in a slightly strangled, high-pitched voice. Ryan duly obliged, and began to replace the tins on the shelf. As he did, the crowd burst into a spontaneous round of applause as Dan's face began to turn increasingly crimson, thanks to the combined discomfort of the physical pain she was inflicting upon him and the accompanying humiliation.

"Good," said Lauren, not relaxing her grip until the final tin was back on the shelf.

"Now leave your trolley and get out," she said, watching with satisfaction as a winded Dan and timid Ryan retreated with their tails between their legs. Once they were a good ten yards away, he turned and shouted,

"I'll get you for this, you bitch."

"So brave, aren't you, shouting back once you're far enough away to feel safe?" she retorted. "Bring it on, any time."

Nothing more was said, as Lauren turned back to the crowd and said, "Now, who wants some tuna?"

Plenty did, and she started to hand the reclaimed packs back to the delighted shoppers.

"Here you go, one pack each, plenty for everyone," she said, enjoying doing her good deed for the day. As she handed out the tins, she noticed one of the supermarket managers standing at the back of the group. Catching his eye, she decided to issue him with a rebuke, too.

"Yes, this is what you should be doing, isn't it, mate? Allowing people to behave like those two just did and not saying anything? It's not a good look, is it."

The manager said nothing and slunk away, just as Kaylee and Charlie came up, having finally made their way into the store. Of Patricia, there was no sign.

"What's going on here, then?" asked Kaylee, who had spotted the end of the altercation from afar and spent the last two minutes fighting her way through the crowd to reach Lauren.

"Oh, just issuing a little local justice, since the management can't be bothered," said Lauren. "Here, do you want some tuna? This is the last four tins."

"Thanks," said Kaylee, putting the tuna into what was a rather spartan trolley compared to some of those she had seen earlier.

"I'm glad to see you're not behaving like some of the animals in here," said Lauren.

"Chance would be a fine thing," said Charlie. "There is hardly anything left. I just saw two young women fighting over the last French stick. I thought they were going to tear each other's hair out. Eventually, they ended up with half each after

92

it broke in two as they were tugging on each end like it was a Christmas cracker. Why are people behaving like this?"

"Because they're scared," said Lauren. "Scared of disappearing, like all the others. And scared for their loved ones, some of whom will already have gone. And on top of all that, scared that if they are left behind, there might not be anything left to eat."

"And right now, scenes like this are doubtless being played out all across the country," said Charlie.

"But why?" said Kaylee. "Why is this happening? None of it makes any sense. Josh said he was going to try and figure it out, but do you think he will?"

"Perhaps it's time to stop trying to make sense of it," said Lauren. "And start preparing for what's to come."

"Which is?" asked Kaylee, with a sense of foreboding.

"Nothing good," she said. "Look, can I stay with you two tonight? My mother's somewhere in the store but I don't think I can bear to spend another night with her. She's bought into all this craziness, lock, stock, and barrel."

"I've got a better suggestion," said Charlie. "There isn't a lot of room at ours, my mum's there as well, remember. Instead, why don't you move into Hannah's place? It's empty now, and you've still got the key, haven't you, Kaylee?"

"I don't know," said Lauren, mulling it over. "It feels wrong somehow, almost as if I'm stepping into a dead woman's shoes."

"She's not dead, and nor is Jess," said Kaylee. "It is vital we continue to believe that. Otherwise we might as well just give up now."

"At least they're out of all this, wherever they are," said Lauren, who could hear shouting coming from a couple of aisles away, and the sound of glass bottles smashing.

"I hope that wasn't coming from the wine aisle," said Charlie. "Mum told me to stock up on the essentials. I class wine as an essential."

"If what I think is on the way does indeed come to pass, you may well need it," said Lauren ominously.

What she had seen in the supermarket had shocked her, though, in hindsight, it was totally predictable. Given how quickly people's behaviour had plummeted already, the consequences for society if the disappearances continued scarcely bore thinking about.

"Come on, let's get what we can and get out of here," urged Kaylee. "Before things turn ugly."

"They are pretty ugly already," said Lauren, at the sound of more breaking glass. "How long before someone gets hurt? Or worse?"

With difficulty, they made their way around the shop, but supplies were hard to come by. Pasta, rice, canned goods, and long-life products had been virtually cleaned out and now shoppers were focusing on the fresh produce. The store had become dangerously crowded, with people all but crushing each other as they squeezed past one another, desperate to get their hands on whatever they could find on the almost depleted shelves.

Lauren had no idea if the store had a capacity, but it had surely been breached. What was the management doing about it? Not a lot, it seemed. Perhaps it was another scenario that had never been envisaged.

The queues at the checkouts were so long now that some people had started to walk out without paying. The lone security guard at the front of the store was powerless to stop them. Once others realised this, they began to copy, and several abandoned the queues and barged their way through the crowds, shouting, jostling, and ramming their trollies into anyone who got in their way.

Contrary to what Lauren had been thinking, the managers were acutely aware of what was going on and were holding a crisis meeting to determine an emergency course of action. The resulting decision came in the form of an announcement over the loudspeaker system.

"Please note that due to unprecedented demand, this store will be closing in five minutes. Please vacate the premises immediately. Do not use the lifts. Also, please do not take any goods with you that you have not paid for. Any person believed to have done so will be reported to the police and prosecuted."

It was just about the worst thing they could have done. The panic buying accelerated into a frenzy now that a time limit had been imposed.

Then, the fire alarm went off. It was the last desperate attempt by the management to clear the store. It worked, but probably not in the way they had intended. In the stampede to the exit, everybody kept tight hold of their trollies and raced for the front door, like a bunch of formula one cars heading into the first corner at the Monaco Grand Prix. Many were swept out through the doors, even if they hadn't intended to leave by that route. They had just become caught up in the unstoppable one-way flow. Getting their shopping back up to their cars on the roof was going to be a challenge.

Charlie, Kaylee, and Lauren had ended up in this tidal wave of shoppers, and were now outside with a trolley of goods they hadn't paid for. At least they had emerged unscathed, unlike some of the stragglers who had fallen and suffered cuts and bruises. It was a miracle nobody had been seriously hurt.

There was no sign of Patricia. Perhaps she had made it back up one of the travellators, which was the only way aside from the lifts to take a trolley up to the top floor.

"This feels a bit dishonest," said Kaylee, as the last few people came out of the store, and the management began to bring down the shutters. "You don't really think they are going to prosecute people, do you?"

96

"Ask if you can go back in and pay if you feel that guilty," said Lauren.

"I don't think they're bothered about the money right now," said Charlie, looking at the panicked faces of the staff through the window who were desperately trying to secure the store.

"Is this really the shape of things to come?" asked Kaylee.

"Believe me, this is only the beginning," said Lauren.

Chapter Seven
July 2023

Lauren's prediction proved to be an accurate one, as the days that followed witnessed the gradual yet undeniable unravelling of the stable world that everyone had previously taken for granted.

Jenna's announcement proved to be ineffective in alleviating the situation. Increased endeavours, such as daily televised briefings aiming to reassure the population, only served to deepen divisions. The people became polarised, forming distinct factions. Some, like Patricia, fervently embraced the alien narrative, while others remained sceptical. Others didn't care. They were more interested in exploiting the situation, in ways that would benefit only themselves.

Those who thought like Patricia became increasingly paranoid, seeking whatever shelter they could find to escape the fictitious aliens. At night, some began to go down into the London Underground, just as their grandparents had during the Blitz. Attempts to stop them were futile, and the remaining commuters who hadn't yet abandoned their jobs found themselves dodging sleepers wrapped in blankets when the trains began running in the mornings.

Those trains would not be running much longer. Air travel had already been grounded and after a series of road accidents, the government felt they had no alternative but to suspend all forms of public transport. Some had argued that trains ought to be allowed to continue because they were already equipped with plenty of safety features to deal with situations where a driver might become incapacitated. There had been a couple of situations already where drivers had vanished but the trains had been brought to a halt automatically when the missing drivers had failed to interact with what was known as the 'dead man's switch'.

The decision to shut down the transport network wasn't taken lightly. It was debated at great length on Thursday morning in the latest of the endless COBR meetings that had taken place since the weekend. The cabinet was facing a difficult choice. The press and public, as well as the rail unions, were putting massive pressure on them to stop the trains, and in the end they capitulated. It was decided that the risk of a fatal accident was too great, despite the safety measures.

The Chancellor of the Exchequer argued vehemently against this, stating that the problems that would be caused by bringing the country to a standstill would far outweigh those of keeping the trains running, but he was shouted down. Jenna was in charge and automatically went against Simon's opinion. She felt it was essential that he was put in his place if she was to make the most of her newfound power.

Jenna had plenty of points with which to back up her argument, not least of which was that if accidents did occur, the emergency services might not be able to cope. They were stretched enough at the best of times, and with over half of their workers either missing or failing to turn up to work, there simply were not enough ambulance drivers available to attend potential accident scenes. It was the same in the hospitals which had become chronically short-staffed, and one thing she knew could threaten her position would be if it was suggested that she was doing anything that could cause the NHS to collapse.

The staff shortages were affecting services and businesses all over the country. As the week wore on, fewer and fewer people were turning up to work. It wasn't just those that had disappeared. Those with family members who had gone missing were too traumatised by their loss to even think about their jobs. Others, increasingly realising the perilous nature of the developing situation, were focused on other priorities and that meant securing enough essential supplies to see them through whatever was happening. Making sure there was a meal on the table that evening was a greater priority than going into the office.

Statisticians pored over the numbers, estimating that approximately 3% of the original population was disappearing each day and that number seemed to remain consistent from day to day. If the trend continued, it would take barely a month for everyone on the planet to have vanished.

As the days passed, those left behind were having to deal with a heady mix of disbelief and fear. The sudden and unexplained vanishing of their friends, family members, and neighbours was fuelling increasing unease and paranoia within communities. There was a growing realisation that their survival, as the infrastructure they had been dependent on their entire lives began to crumble all around them, was very much at risk.

100

The great unanswered question remained 'why'? There was no pattern to any of it that supported any attempt to fashion a plausible explanation. The phenomenon did not discriminate between young, old, black, white, rich, or poor. It took people at random and in equal measure across the world. There was no country unaffected that could be accused of developing some kind of super weapon to depopulate the rest of the world.

There was simply no answer. After a few days, even the official alien story began to wear thin, though some still clung to it, helped by faked social media clips purportedly showing the UFOs in action.

By now it had been established that it was the entire animal kingdom, from the largest beasts to the tiniest single-celled creatures that were affected. All were disappearing at the same rate which explained what had happened to Arthur Tuddenham's cows. When he had been in the station complaining about cattle rustlers on the day it had all begun, it had all been part of the phenomenon.

Some who did not believe the alien story looked to religion as a possible explanation. Many adopted the view that the end of days had indeed come, as espoused by Bob the Bible Basher's exhortations in the town centre. Many turned to prayer and repentance in the hope that if the time had come to ascend to the Rapture, they would be among those selected. Invariably, none of this made any difference. People continued to disappear at the same rate, regardless of what they believed.

Those hiding underground or building makeshift bunkers in their gardens would have realised it was a waste of time if they had known that navy officers on submarines, deep in the ocean, were also disappearing, as were the creatures that lived down there in the murky depths. The oceans were emptying of fish too, as the few trawlers still operating discovered as they found yields to be increasingly disappointing. There was nowhere to hide, wherever you were on the planet, but people still tried. When sleepers on the Underground disappeared in full view of others around them, those left behind simply stole their belongings and then went to a deeper station the following evening.

Josh's visit to Professor Hamilton on Monday had revealed nothing. They talked about the situation all day and then, with all the pubs shut, continued over a bottle of Hamilton's favourite malt long into the night. They came up with no end of clever theories, but when they broke each one down and analysed it, they ended up dismissing them all.

He stayed in Oxford for a few days, helping his mentor tinker around with his various devices but everything they did was fruitless. A few nights trying to keep pace with Hamilton's love of whisky left him feeling distinctly rough, and it wasn't just that. Life in Oxford was becoming increasingly fraught, and by Friday morning he had decided it was time to go back home while he still could.

Figuring out how he was going to get back from Oxford was problematic. Josh didn't drive so was reliant on public transport, and by then there wasn't any. It had all been suspended by Jenna's decree. Private car travel was also supposedly forbidden but there were still some vehicles on the roads. No one seemed interested in stopping them. He thought there might be a chance he could persuade a taxi driver to take him, but there wasn't a cab to be found. They had all given up.

Oxford on Friday morning was quiet and had more than a whiff of the post-apocalyptic about it. He had seen it going downhill over a few days, and by now all the shops were closed. Despite that, there were plenty of people out on the streets. Some were wandering in a dazed state, eerily reminiscent of the many zombie apocalypse movies he had watched as a teenager. Others, more aware, were eyeing people up and giving off a distinct hint of menace. It left Josh eager to get out of the city as soon as possible.

After bidding Hamilton goodbye, he began walking up Banbury Road towards Summertown, keeping well out of other people's way. All was quiet until he got close to the shopping area when he heard the unwelcome sound of shattering glass. It had come from a Costa Coffee on the right-hand side of the street, just up ahead, which it appeared was being raided.

He had seen a few places with their windows put through already. Things must be getting bad if people were that desperate for a coffee, he thought. Or were they just after money? That seemed a bit pointless to him. If things continued as they were, money was going to be of no use to anyone.

The atmosphere was causing him to feel distinctly unsafe, and up ahead he could see abandoned cars blocking the road, one of which had been burnt out. It was beginning to resemble a war zone. Was he going to be able to get home unscathed? It was a hell of a long walk, probably a good fifteen miles.

Then he remembered that he had passed a bicycle shop a few minutes earlier. He retraced his steps and discovered that this too had fallen victim to the growing crime wave. The door had been kicked in and was now hanging loosely off its hinges.

"Hello?" he called, stepping inside. "Anyone home?"

The shop was a mess, where much of the merchandise had been smashed up for no reason he could see other than mindless vandalism. Among the wreckage was a till tray, which presumably had been emptied by whoever had broken in. Well, he hoped they enjoyed their ill-gotten gains because as far he could see there was nowhere left to spend them. But that wasn't what he had come for.

He couldn't spend his money either which left him in a bit of a dilemma. He had come for a bicycle but there was nobody here to sell him one. He did have some cash on him, but it seemed pointless leaving it on the counter for the owner because the next person to come in here would doubtless steal it. The only thing to do was to take a bicycle and come back later and pay when all this business was resolved, if it ever was.

Fortunately, despite the state of the shop, there were still a few undamaged bicycles to choose from. That demonstrated just how little foresight people had. With most fuel-powered forms of transport out of commission, the good old-fashioned pushbike was just what was needed to get about.

He chose a red mountain bike, which might be useful if he had to negotiate any difficult terrain, and took it outside. Then, he got on and started pedalling through Summertown. As he did, he was shocked to see that the whole area had been well and truly trashed. Thankfully, there was no sign of the coffee shop raiders and most of the other people around ignored him. However, as he passed the smashed-up local BBC Radio station building, the menacing figure of a man in leathers and a motorcycle helmet strode into the road and tried to block his path. Josh tried to steer around him, at which point the aggressor produced a baseball bat, seemingly out of nowhere, and took a swing at him.

He swerved desperately to the right, barely avoiding the attack, and almost falling off the bike in the process. Then he was in the clear and sprinting away at high speed, spurred on by a mix of adrenaline and fear. For the first time, it hit home just how precarious the situation was. The world was teetering on the edge of anarchy.

Once he was out of immediate danger, he slowed down a little and looked around him. There was no sign that the man with the baseball bat was following him, and now he was away from the shops, the streets were spookily quiet. However, there was no shortage of evidence that there had been trouble in the local area. At one point, he saw copious amounts of blood splattered all over an advertising hoarding on the side of a bus shelter, highlighting once again how simply by being outside, he was putting his life at stake.

Wherever he looked he saw reminders that the safe and stable world he had always taken for granted was being rapidly stripped away. His brief encounter with the leather-clad man was not likely to be a one-off. There could be all manner of dangerous people roaming the area, resorting to whatever measures they deemed necessary to survive.

As he approached the slip road to the A34, he came across the scene of a major accident. Cars were strewn haphazardly across the road, with twisted metal and shattered glass scattered all over the road. Josh manoeuvred his borrowed bicycle carefully through the wreckage, not wanting to get a puncture. It hadn't crossed his mind to pick up a repair kit when he had been back in the shop.

The usually busy dual carriageway stretched before him, devoid of the bustling traffic it had hosted just a few days before when he had travelled into Oxford on the bus. That meant he would not have to worry about any traffic coming up behind him for the first stretch. The pile-up he had just picked his way through had rendered the northbound carriageway impassable. He had never seen anyone riding a bicycle on this road. It was too dangerous. But today, he had it all to himself.

Things were different on the southbound side, which was still negotiable. Occasionally, the odd driver raced past recklessly. He saw one in a smart suit in what was probably his company Mercedes, looking as if he was heading off for an important business meeting. *Good luck with that*, thought Josh. The man was deluding himself if he thought wherever he was going was more important than what was happening to the world.

He was thankful for the central reservation which protected him from traffic coming the other way. Even so, his heart rate picked up every time a vehicle approached, wary that any encounter now could be dangerous. He was also concerned that soon he would pass the Islip turn and then there would be nothing to stop vehicles joining his side of the carriageway.

Thankfully, very few did, and on the three occasions he did hear a car approaching, he pulled off to the side of the road. The first two ignored him, but the third, filled with a group of young men, veered dangerously close to him. One of them threw an empty beer bottle at him, which only just missed, as one of the others shouted "bike wanker" at him through the open window.

As he pedalled further there were no more cars and he became aware of how silent his surroundings were. He couldn't even hear any birdsong. What was going to happen to chicks in nests whose parents never returned? It was one of the things he had and Hamilton had talked about. The entire ecosystem would be starting to break down by now.

Then he saw something in the distance up ahead, which prompted him to stop and get off the bike. He could make out that the carriageway had been coned off and a large green lorry emblazoned with the logo of one of the major supermarket chains had stopped in front of it. Parked next to that was a large black Range Rover.

He was at least half a mile away but watched as a couple of men got out of the Range Rover and beckoned the driver down from his truck. Josh couldn't hear what was being said, he was too far away for that. He watched as the driver was led around to the back of the truck, which he then opened.

Shortly afterwards, he saw him fall to the ground, just before the air was shattered by the sound of the gunshot that had felled him.

Chapter Eight
July 2023

Seeing the man fall before he heard the gunshot seemed strange, but with light travelling faster than sound, it was perfectly logical sense. But Josh didn't have time to dwell on the physics. What he had just witnessed had been a watershed moment in the continuing collapse of civilisation. There was no way he was going any further on this road. His overriding priority now was to get out of sight before the villains who had just murdered the lorry driver spotted him.

He scrambled over to the boundary at the edge of the carriageway and through a gap in the bordering trees, hoping the killers had not seen him. He planned to take a detour through the surrounding fields and find safe passage onto the road further ahead. Or preferably, avoid it altogether.

His decision to choose a mountain bike had been a wise one as he would not have been able to navigate the rough terrain of the fields on a standard road bike. The wet summer had left the ground soft and muddy, and despite being young and fit, he found getting through it was hard work. The sound of some sort of explosion in the distance behind him spurred him on, giving him a renewed determination to get home safely. He was sweating and out of breath as he continued, and desperate for a drink. Water was another thing he hadn't thought to bring.

Looking back, he could see a plume of smoke rising, a couple of miles back on the road he had just left. That settled it, he was not going anywhere near the main roads again. Instead, he planned to get on the back lanes and risk getting back to the town via one of the small villages. The country lane he made his way onto was clear, giving him a brief respite from the horrors he had left behind.

When he reached the village, he made his way cautiously, scrutinising everything in front of him in detail and ready to take evasive action at the first sign of danger. But things in the village appeared reassuringly normal compared to what he had seen earlier. He even saw a couple of pensioners walking their dogs, blissfully unaware that people were being shot for food just a few miles away.

After leaving the village he only had a couple of miles left to get back to his hometown, but his tribulations were not over yet. Rounding a tight turn in the road, bordered by trees on either side, he came across another confrontational scene, right in front of him. This time he had no choice but to get involved.

A small Kia had stopped in the middle of the narrow lane, and a man was wrestling with the driver, a young Asian woman, through the car window. She was screaming at him to get away as he attempted to open the door and drag her from the car.

Fortuitously, the attacker was so preoccupied with his attempted assault he did not see Josh approaching which enabled him to dismount from his bike, unobserved. Looking around, he grabbed a loose rock about the size of a tennis ball from beside the road and whacked the assailant over the head with it. The blow knocked him out cold and he immediately sank to the floor.

The young woman behind the wheel looked familiar but despite his heroic rescue, she didn't turn to thank him. She quickly put the car into gear, preparing to drive off. Josh saw that she was gasping for breath as she did, a sign of distress from her ordeal. Perhaps she thought he was another potential attacker, and who could blame her with the way things had been panning out?

"Don't be afraid," said Josh quickly, through the open window, desperate to assure her he was not a threat. "I'm not going to hurt you and this scumbag is out cold."

She paused, leaving the engine running and then turned to look him full in the face for the first time. Now he knew who she was.

"Thank you," she said, in a voice he also recognised. "Are you sure he's unconscious?"

Josh looked down at the prone body of the man he had struck, sprawled face down at his feet.

"Yes, he won't be going anywhere for a while. My name's Josh, by the way."

"Seema," she replied, beginning to breathe more slowly as her fear subsided.

"I thought it was," said Josh. "I've heard you on the radio. And you used to write for our local paper."

"I certainly did," she replied. "Such a shame it went bust. Local papers used to be the heart and soul of communities but no one wants them anymore."

"Listen, what are you doing out here by yourself?" asked Josh. "It's getting incredibly dangerous."

"Don't I know it," she said. "I'm trying to get back to Oxford. I've been visiting my dad in Aylesbury, but he's gone now."

"Disappeared?" asked Josh.

"Yes, just like all the others. I couldn't go back to Oxford on the A418. It's blocked. So I thought I would try and make my way via the back roads."

"Believe me, you don't want to go back to Oxford. I've just come from there. It's hell. You see this guy here? There are plenty more like him back there – and worse."

"I shouldn't have stopped but he was lying in the road. I thought he was hurt. When I stopped the car he jumped up and tried to grab hold of me through the window."

"Did he say anything? Do you think he was trying to steal the car?"

"I don't think so. I think he meant to sexually assault me. He went straight for my breasts with one hand while he fumbled for the door handle with the other."

"Bloody hell, I can't believe things have sunk to this level of savageness so quickly. I've seen some terrible things today."

"So, where are you headed now?" asked Seema. "Can I give you a lift anywhere? Safety in numbers and all that."

"To the nearest town, a mile or two back that way. I have friends there. Perhaps you should come with me. It's far too dangerous to go back to Oxford. Do you have family there?"

"No, it's where I work. I was hoping to get back to Radio Oxford. I thought maybe I could do some good, put something out over the airwaves to calm the people. I mean, we're meant to be under a news blackout, but it barely matters now, does it?"

"I went past the BBC building in Summertown earlier. The windows have all been smashed in and the place ransacked. Believe me, there's nothing for you there."

"That would explain why I can't pick them up on the radio," she said. "I sort of suspected something like that might have happened but I wanted to see for myself. I've got a curious nature. I guess that's part of the reason I became a journalist."

"Oh, they're off the air, for good, I would think. You would be far safer coming with me."

"Then what?"

"We'll figure that out when we get there but we need to get off these roads sooner rather than later."

"Hop in, then. You'll have to direct me."

Josh propped his bike up against a tree and hopped in the passenger seat. He felt quite sad leaving the bike behind. He would never have made it this far without it. But Seema's Kia was small, and there wouldn't be enough room for it.

"Do you mind if I make a couple of quick calls before we go?" he asked. "I need to check where my friends are and that we have somewhere safe to go."

"Go ahead," said Seema, "but don't be too long. We don't want that guy waking up again."

"I just hope the phones are still working," replied Josh.

Thankfully, they were. First, he called his parents to check on their well-being. They confirmed they were safe and well on their holiday down in the West Country. It didn't sound as if things were too bad down there. They had hired a campervan for the trip and were parked up in a remote area near Falmouth. They seemed oblivious to what was going on and he advised them to stay put. They would be a lot safer down there than they would be trying to get back home.

Next, he phoned Charlie, who explained that Lauren was still staying at Hannah's house and he suggested they all meet up there. From the brief conversation, it sounded like things were getting bad in the town too and so it proved when Seema drove her Kia slowly through the outskirts. Once a bustling hub of activity, it was now deserted. Abandoned cars and signs of vandalism here and there bore witness to the lawlessness that had befallen this place too.

Seema drove an electric car, something he was glad of as it glided quietly through the streets. The less noise they made the better.

Charlie and Kaylee had spent the past few days holed up with his mother, Sarah, and they had not left home since returning from the supermarket at the start of the week. They had been among the more fortunate ones, at least bringing home a few supplies when they had been swept outside after the fire alarm had gone off. The house had been well stocked with food beforehand anyway so they hadn't had to go out for more. Sarah worked in a bakery, but that had been cleaned out at the same time as the supermarket. The owner had closed it on the same day, declaring that it would remain so until further notice.

Since then, the three of them had not dared to leave her small semi-detached home. They had no fear of the fictional alien threat but it was what was going on out on the streets they were afraid of. Unrest had been growing, particularly at night.

When Charlie said that he and Kaylee were going to Hannah's house, Sarah was dead set against it. She feared both for their safety outside and her own, being left alone at home.

Kaylee came up with the solution. She had been worrying about her own family but had avoided going around to her house. She and her sister did not get along and never had. Her parents didn't get on either and there had been many times she had suspected they might be on the brink of divorce. It had been a relief to get away from it at eighteen when she had gone to university.

When she called home, her father, Phil, informed her that her mother had become another statistic in the growing toll of disappearances. Her sister was not there either but that was because she had gone to a stay with friends in Manchester at the weekend and had not come back. She had phoned home to let her father know she was safe but had no way of getting back now the trains had stopped running.

That left Phil on his own so Kaylee suggested that he and Sarah stayed together for protection while they were out. Phil agreed, but he wasn't happy about Charlie and Kaylee going out either after he ran into trouble on his way over. Both parents didn't understand why they felt the need to go anywhere at all, but Kaylee made up a white lie about Lauren running out of food and that they needed to take her some. They grabbed a few things and put them in a bag to make it convincing and then left despite Sarah and Phil's protestations.

Lauren had not returned to her mother's house all week. She felt a lot more secure where she was than she would have done back home. Hannah was very security conscious and had good sturdy locks on all the doors. She had fitted them not long after moving in, aware from her profession just how important home security was.

Technically the house wasn't Hannah's, it was Peter's and there was still evidence of him everywhere even if he had not been present for a long time. This included his razor and shaving foam which were sitting on the windowsill behind the bathroom sink, waiting for his return. Now, when Lauren looked at them she had to wonder if he ever would. Would any of them ever return from the unknown place to which they had been whisked?

Lauren mulled over these thoughts as she was cleaning her teeth on Friday morning. It felt stuffy in the bathroom so she tried to open the frosted glass window, eager to let in some cool air. It was stiff and difficult to move, partly due to some ivy which was creeping across and starting to attach itself to the window frame.

The ivy brought a disturbing thought to mind which she broached with Charlie and Kaylee when they arrived.

"What's going to happen to the world if everybody disappears and never returns? How long will it take for nature to reclaim the planet? If we were to return in a thousand years, would all trace of humanity have been erased, consumed by vegetation?"

"Oh, I think it would take considerably less time than that," said Kaylee. "Perhaps this is all Mother Nature's way of reclaiming the planet. We've been trashing it long enough. Maybe something like this was inevitable."

"Yes, but would it?" asked Charlie. "All animal life is vanishing, including the insects. Earth lives in a delicate balance between animal and vegetable. We breathe in oxygen and breathe out carbon dioxide. Plants do the opposite. What happens if you remove one side of that equation? And regarding the plants, how are they to be pollinated without the birds and the bees?"

"By the wind?" suggested Kaylee.

"I'm not sure that alone will be enough," said Charlie. "The whole system is reliant on all the constituent parts of it working in harmony."

"Well, plants managed alright for millions of years before animals evolved," said Kaylee. "I'm sure they would adapt."

"It's weird imagining a world devoid of people, isn't it?" said Lauren. "Weeds sprouting up everywhere, then mighty forests."

"That's unless the aliens move in first," said Charlie.

"Ah, yes, the lovely aliens," said Lauren. "How could I forget? My mum still thinks they're real, you know."

It was at that moment that the doorbell rang and Lauren went to answer. Wisely, she looked through the peephole first and was relieved to see Josh on the doorstep. She was surprised to see that he wasn't alone, particularly when she opened the door to see who was accompanying him.

"Josh," she said. "And it's Seema, isn't it? We've never met, but you're a bit of a local celebrity. I'm feeling a bit star-struck!"

"Stop it, you'll make me blush," said Seema, taking an instant liking to Lauren's friendly persona.

"I met her on the way here," said Josh. "She was being attacked by some pervert. It's not safe out there. Let's get in quickly and get this door bolted. I don't think anyone saw us arrive, but you can't take any chances."

At the kitchen table, Seema was soon being quizzed by the rest of the team. They were under the impression that if anyone knew what was going on, a BBC journalist would.

"But you must have some inkling as to what is causing all this," said Charlie.

"Believe me, I don't," said Seema. "And from what I've seen, nobody else does either. What you see in those endless crisis briefings on television is purely the acting Prime Minister's attempts to try and quell the growing panic. I don't trust her at all. She's a slippery character, by all accounts."

"Well, she's failing miserably on that front," said Josh. "We've seen enough examples out there already. The country is descending into complete anarchy. The shops are shut, no food supplies are getting through and that's creating a desperate situation where people are fighting to the death to get their hands on what food remains."

"That's a pretty grim assessment," said Kaylee. "Couldn't those of us who remain all work together to manage what resources we have without having to descend into violence?"

"You're being idealistic, Kaylee," said Josh. "Yes, there are plenty of people who would see that as the ideal solution but unfortunately there will be many that won't. With no authority, and therefore no deterrent, those with less than honourable intentions than ourselves will have no hesitation in riding roughshod over the rest of us. That has been the way throughout human history."

"Yes, but we are a civilised society now," said Charlie. "We're beyond that sort of thing, surely?"

"You are being naïve, Charlie," said Josh. "And you, Kaylee. Hang around here and see how quickly your civilised society descends into barbarism."

"I have to say, I agree with Josh," said Lauren. "I think we are in deep trouble."

"So what's your solution?" asked Seema.

"We get out of town, and fast," said Josh. "I think it won't be long until gangs of marauders start going house to house in search of food. And I don't expect them to ring the doorbell and ask politely."

"You honestly think they would break in? Food can't be that scarce, surely?" asked Kaylee.

"Yes, there are fewer people around to eat it, for a start," added Charlie. "And more and more disappearing every day."

"Doesn't matter," said Josh. "Once society has broken down, cash will become worthless. Food and resources will be the new currency. Whoever controls the supply of it will hold the power."

"And for those who don't have any?"

"Then things get really bad," said Josh. "You don't even want to think about what people might do if they are desperate enough. I've seen it already. Put it this way, it might not just be food, as in tins of beans, they might be looking for if they broke in here."

"What do you mean?" said Charlie.

"I'd prefer not to spell it out," said Josh, looking around the table. "The ladies might find it unpalatable."

"Oh, don't be so old-fashioned, Josh. We're not delicate flowers that need protecting by our menfolk," said Lauren. "Well, I'm not anyway and I doubt Seema is either. Spit it out."

"Very well," said Josh. "If the worst kind of people broke in here they might very kill us all. And then cook us and eat us."

"Urgh, no, surely not," said Kaylee.

"Oh, and they would probably rape the three of you first," he said, looking at Kaylee, Lauren and Seema.

"Josh, I can't believe what you're saying," said Kaylee. "This is just horrific scaremongering and it's not helping."

"No, it isn't. It's a realistic worst-case scenario. I saw the driver of a food lorry accosted and shot dead by two men on my way here earlier."

"Seriously?" asked Charlie. "Already?"

"Yes, and Seema here might well have been raped if I hadn't intervened."

"Believe me, I'd have put up a good fight," said Seema.

"And how many more people are there like those I saw today roaming around looking for trouble? That's why we need to get away from here as soon as we can."

"So where do you suggest we go?" asked Lauren.

"Anywhere rural. The more remote the better. The fewer people there are around the better. I spoke to my parents down in Cornwall earlier. They are in the middle of nowhere and seem barely aware of what's going on."

"Where are they staying?" asked Seema.

"They hired a campervan from Murray's place, over near Kirtlington," replied Josh. "They're all kitted out and self-sufficient. It's probably the best thing they could have done, even though they couldn't have known what was on the way."

"You're not suggesting we try and travel all the way to Cornwall, are you?" asked Lauren.

"Of course not. Just somewhere in the country where we can defend ourselves. A deserted farmhouse or something like that. But we need some way of getting there and a campervan would be ideal."

"And if we do find somewhere in the country, what are we going to do for food when we get there?" asked Kaylee.

"We take what we can find before we leave town," said Josh. "And then look for more."

"Where?" said Charlie. "I hardly think we're going to find a massive Tesco out in the wilderness, stocked up with everything we need."

"There are such things as trees and bushes that have fruit growing on them," said Josh. "And fish in the river, maybe, if they haven't all vanished. Does anyone here know how to catch them?"

He was met with a sea of blank faces.

"I don't know how to fish, but I know where there's a stack of it to be had," said Lauren. "My mother's a conspiracy theorist and a prepper. She's been convinced Western civilisation is about to fall apart for years. My bedroom is full of tins of tuna."

"She was right," said Charlie.

"Yes, but probably not in the way she was expecting," replied Lauren. "Though whether she is willing to part with any of it is another matter."

"Not even to help out her own daughter?" asked Seema.

"We don't exactly see eye to eye."

"Right, whatever we do manage to take with us, we are still going to need to go somewhere where we can find more," said Charlie.

"It's coming up to harvest time," said Kaylee. "So like Josh said there will be plenty of fruit and veg about. I'm sure even we with our pampered modern lifestyles can pick a few strawberries. And what about wheat? Could we make flour from it?"

"I think that might be pushing it," said Josh. "Do any of us here know how to make bread? And I mean from scratch, not just buying the ingredients from Tesco and chucking them into a bread maker. Could you find and process all the ingredients in their natural state? Then bake them, in a situation where perhaps we might not have any gas or electricity?"

They sat pondering the reality of how they would manage even a simple task, such as producing a loaf of bread.

"We're helpless, aren't we?" said Charlie.

"I think we're going to have to learn to do a lot of things very quickly," replied Josh. "And be realistic about what is and what isn't achievable."

"I suggest we sit down and plan it all out very carefully before we go rushing off anywhere," said Seema.

"Agreed," said Lauren. "Shall we get started?"

The group around the table nodded their heads in acknowledgement but without a huge degree of enthusiasm.

They all knew what a fragile situation they were in, and it set a sombre tone.

Chapter Nine
July 2023

If, as Josh had suggested, the more remote the place, the safer it was, then the opposite was also true. In Britain, there was no more dangerous place to be right now than London. In deprived areas of high population density such as tower blocks, feral gangs had taken control, going from door to door and taking whatever they could find.

There was still some semblance of normality in more upmarket areas, but nowhere would be safe for long. It was inevitable that the drug dealers and other criminals who controlled the most downmarket areas would seize this new opportunity with both hands and spread out, seeking richer pickings. There was no longer anyone to stop them.

Even the secure environment of Westminster was beginning to come under threat. Jenna's attempts to control the situation were failing and many citizens gravitated there in search of answers. The populace was hungry and it was angry, a dangerous combination, as the rulers of France had discovered in 1789.

A large crowd had formed in front of the black iron gate which restricted public access to Downing Street. Two beleaguered policemen were doing their best to keep the people back but the sheer weight of numbers, all shouting and demanding to be let through, was becoming increasingly intimidating.

Less than a hundred yards away in the cabinet office, Dominic was chairing a last desperate meeting to try to maintain some sort of control of the situation. The mood was very much one of hopelessness as most of them had reached the inevitable conclusion that there was nothing more that could be done. They were now at the stage of damage limitation and ensuring their personal safety.

Jenna was still ruling the roost and had been exchanging her usual war of words with Simon. The only other attendee was the energy secretary, James Brookes, who had been painting a bleak picture of the current situation for Britain's power grid. As for the psychologists, they had been dispensed with. The game was well and truly up when it came to trying to bamboozle the public so they were now surplus to requirements.

"We are struggling to maintain the energy supply," said James. "Less than half the workforce showed up yesterday. Today, by all reports it is down to a third. In my considered opinion, this will probably be the final day we can keep things operational."

"And then what?" asked Jenna.

"Then, the power grid grinds to a halt. No electricity, no gas, nothing."

"But we can switch it back on in the future, right? And the renewables will still work?"

"It's not as simple as that," said James. "These things need to be carefully managed. If just left unattended, the

127

consequences could be catastrophic. The power grid depends on a delicate balance of supply and demand. When parts of it go offline, the remaining load could overwhelm the grid, potentially damaging transformers, and other grid infrastructure beyond repair."

"Yes, well, it's not like we're going to need any of it again, is it?" said Jenna. "There won't be anyone here to use it."

"We don't know that for sure," said Simon. "Someone might come up with the solution to all this and if we've fried the only means we've got of generating energy in the future, what then?"

"And that's not the only problem we've got," said James. "It might not be catastrophic if we turn off the wind turbines, but have you thought about the nuclear power stations? What happens to all that radioactive material? It's a potential disaster waiting to happen."

"Turn them off as well then," suggested Jenna.

"You can't just turn off a nuclear power station," said an exasperated James. "They take years to decommission."

"But you must have made contingency plans for such a situation?" asked Simon.

"We have emergency protocols in place," said James. "In case we ever needed to shut as much of it off as possible at short notice – say in the event of a solar flare or something like that. Assuming we got enough warning, which is a big assumption."

"Then do it now," said Jenna. "While you've still got enough people in place to do it."

"Do you honestly think that is a good idea?" asked Simon. "The people are restless enough as it is. When the lights go out, that will be the final straw. There will be riots."

"There practically are already," said Dominic.

"Can't spin your way out of this one, can you, Dom?" said Simon. "The man with all the answers, isn't that what you call yourself?"

"I don't see you offering any solutions," replied Dominic.

"I still say we should have put the army on the streets and told them to shoot looters on sight," said Jenna.

"Well, you would," said Simon.

The door to the cabinet office opened, and a parliamentary undersecretary came in and spoke to Dominic in hushed tones. After she had gone, he immediately turned on a large television screen on the wall which showed the crowd on the verge of storming the gates at the end of Downing Street.

"That's our cue to leave," he said. "We need to get out of here. James, get on to your people and tell them to shut down as much of the grid as possible. As for the rest of us, I think you'll all agree, it's time to put Operation Eden into play."

This had already been discussed earlier in the meeting. He was referring to plans to retreat to a secret underground bunker beneath Parliament. There were already a set of Cabinet War Rooms below which had been used in the last century, and the existence of these had been public knowledge since the 1980s. However, there was an additional facility that had remained secret. It had been commissioned by former Prime Minister Anthony Eden during the Cold War and was one of several such boltholes created across the country for use if the worst happened.

Most of the people working in Downing Street did not even know of its existence. Only a handful of senior ministers were aware of it, plus, of course, the skeleton staff needed to maintain it. That left an odd situation where some of the cleaners, who had of course signed the Official Secrets Act, knew all about it, whereas many self-important MPs did not.

It was kept clean and stocked up with fresh food, water and all the other supplies that would be required to keep the occupants alive underground for a lengthy period. Until today, it had never been needed, but for the remaining ministers and their families it would now provide sanctuary.

The bunker was accessible from the cellars of both Number 10 and 11, via security doors constructed of reinforced steel. These were designed to withstand various threats, including explosions, seismic activity, and any hostile physical attempts to gain entry. Such attempts could be monitored from within via advanced security systems, including surveillance cameras, motion sensors, and perimeter barriers to detect and deter potential invaders. There was even weaponry in the form of concealed artillery, should it ever be required.

It was designed to be completely self-sufficient, with backup power generators capable of providing electricity for an extended period. It also had its own water piped from underground wells using purification and filtration systems to ensure a sustainable supply of clean water.

Everything else, from food storage to fresh air circulation and waste management, had been planned meticulously. It was intended that the bunker could sustain up to fifty people for a minimum of one year.

It also contained advanced communication systems to maintain contact with the outside world and coordinate government operations, not that it seemed there would be much use for that on this occasion. As far as Jenna was concerned, as soon as the power grid was shut off, that would be the end of her responsibilities to the outside world. After that, it would be all about prolonging her life in comfort as long as possible. The mood of the crowd currently attempting to gain access to Downing Street looked murderous, going by the pictures on TV. She was under no illusions as to her likely fate should she be caught.

The order was issued and the key personnel on site began to make their way down to the bunker. This included Simon's family from Number 11, and Jenna's husband and two kids whom she had hastily moved into Number 10, just two days ago, after her sudden rise to power.

The plans in place dictated that in the event of Project Eden being activated, everyone needed to be inside the bunker within ten minutes. It looked as if it would barely be enough. The footage on the television was showing that the angry rioters had now overwhelmed the gate and were pouring into Downing Street. By then, there was nobody left in the conference room to see it. Dominic, Jenna, and the others were already on their way down to the bunker, escorted by two army officers. They had appeared seemingly from nowhere once the order to activate Project Eden had been given.

Both soldiers were armed, as it was their number one priority to protect their leader at all costs in this eventuality. Dominic, however, was confident that their weapons would not be needed. He had seen the bunker in operation during a trial run and he knew that there was no way these invaders would be able to gain access to it, no matter how many of them flooded into the building.

James was still on his mobile phone issuing the instructions to shut down the power grid as he descended the stairs towards the bunker. Whether or not he would be successful, he did not know. Chains of command were breaking down everywhere and he just hoped there were enough conscientious people still in place to do what needed to be done.

In addition to the external threat from the crowd trying to get into Number 10, confrontations had arisen internally. The army personnel in charge of the operation had orders to escort certain individuals but not others. Hundreds of people worked in Downing Street, though not all of them were present today. The workforce had been decimated like everywhere else. But there were still enough onsite who were not on the list, and when they found out they were being abandoned, they realised the mortal peril they were in.

Many, who had until a few minutes before been completely unaware of the bunker's existence, tried to blag or force their way inside. They quickly had to abandon those ideas when they were stopped in their tracks by khaki-clad soldiers toting machine guns who made it clear that no one was getting in without authorisation. Turned away, they discovered that they had nowhere to run. By now, the protestors were hammering on the iconic black front door, which was swiftly broken down, leaving the remaining staff facing an incensed crowd with a taste for blood.

Deserted by their leaders, and attacked by those who deemed them responsible for their plight, these remaining workers were cannon fodder for the stampeding hordes that were now flooding into the building. They were beaten and then trampled underfoot as the crowd kept surging forward, hundreds of them. There wasn't any real purpose to their invasion anymore. All they did was vent their anger by smashing and destroying everything in sight. Some took great pleasure in destroying the portraits on the wall of past Prime Ministers, of whichever political persuasions they did not agree with.

Some who had been fortunate enough to secure a place in the bunker were watching developments above them in horror, via CCTV. Jenna, however, was not perturbed in the slightest. These rampaging fools couldn't hurt her, safe in her

133

bolthole. As for the staff who had taken the brunt of the onslaught, in her opinion they only had themselves to blame. She was an important person and she was safe, whereas they were unimportant and therefore dispensable. It was their own fault for not working harder at their lives. Then they might have been important enough to be down here with her.

But they weren't and had paid the price. As for those that had joined her down below, she now had absolute power over them, backed up by the army. Under emergency conditions, she had the power of life and death over everybody. If anyone challenged her, it was within her rights to have them dealt with, in any manner she saw fit. The likes of Simon were going to have to learn to defer to her orders. She would keep Dominic sweet – she had seen in the past how dangerous an enemy he could be – but the rest of them? They would do as they were told.

She smiled, relishing the prospect. For the remainder of her time down here, she intended to live like a queen with her husband and daughters enjoying a similar level of luxury. After all, what was the point of having power if you couldn't make the most of it? An opportunity had come her way and she had seized it. So what if she had only recently lost the leadership election against the now-missing Prime Minister? The result had been a travesty, in her opinion. He hadn't deserved to win, she had, and now whether it be through divine intervention or any other reason, justice had been served. She was here, and he was not.

The violent scenes that had played out upstairs were being repeated in varying degrees across every major city in the world. The White House, the Reichstag and even the Kremlin were being besieged. It was the same story everywhere. People wanted answers and they wanted food and none was forthcoming. This heady combination of rage and hunger was lethal and barely a week after Jake Rogers had been the first to disappear, civilisation in the developed world had effectively fallen.

In smaller settlements, things had not declined to the same extent, but nowhere was unaffected. Many people simply didn't know what they should do next. Those who had managed to stash away enough food for a few weeks stayed holed up in their homes, but it was with a great sense of unease. They knew just how vulnerable they were.

Remarkably, Richard Kent had managed to get through the first week of lockdown with the pub still secure but he knew he was living on borrowed time. His initial reluctance to close his business had soon subsided when he saw from the windows what was going on outside. The Red Lion was an old building with thick stone walls and a heavy oak front door, but he knew that wouldn't be enough to protect him and Debs if someone smashed the windows. He could see from his bedroom above the pub that this had already happened to several other businesses on the main street.

On Friday morning, a week after it all started, he woke up to discover that he was alone. Debs had gone to wherever all the others had gone. He was now alone in a pub full of booze, plus freezers full of food. He had been knocking back the drink all week, not wanting to let it go to waste and to help cope with the situation. Debs had scolded him over it but now she was gone, he figured he might as well carry on. Either he would be taken soon too, or someone would break into the pub and that wasn't a prospect he relished. Either way, the drink would dull whatever pain was coming.

At the weekend, somebody did try to get in, but not via the front door. Kent was sitting morosely at the bar on his own when he heard a loud and insistent banging coming from the back gate. He ignored it for a while in the hope that they would go away but they proved to be remarkably persistent. Eventually, he decided to go out and try to scare the person off. It was probably an unwise thing to do but why change the habit of a lifetime?

Venturing into the deserted beer garden, he headed towards the double gates at the rear of the premises where the potential intruder was now rattling the gate back and forth in frustration. Kent was confident whoever it was would never get it open or be able to climb it. The gates were six feet tall and made of thick, smooth wooden panels.

"Who's there?" demanded Kent, attempting to scare them off. "For your information, I'm armed and I'm not afraid to shoot anyone who tries to break in here."

"You? Armed?" came a sarcastic and familiar voice from the other side of the gate. "I doubt they ever let you get your hands on a gun even when you were a detective inspector. You'd probably have accidentally shot yourself."

"Andy!" exclaimed Kent. "What are you doing here?"

136

"I want a drink, what do you think I'm doing here? And don't give me all that I'm closed because of the lockdown bollocks. Nobody's taking any notice of that anymore."

Kent considered for a moment. Andy was a pain in the arse but even his company was preferable to being alone. And with the current situation, safety in numbers might be the best option.

"I don't know if you've noticed in your booze-addled state, but the whole country's descending into anarchy. I'm not closed because of any government edict. I'm closed because if I opened the front door I'd be mobbed. Sooner or later, I reckon that's going to happen anyway, but if you agree to help me defend the place, yes you can come in."

"Sounds good to me," said Andy, as Kent unlocked the gate, cautiously peering around it to see if anyone had seen them but it was all quiet. The rear of the pub backed onto an alley which didn't go anywhere other than to the back of the properties, so it wasn't used as a thoroughfare.

"I take it you've got plenty of beer left," said Andy, as Kent led the way back inside.

"It's a pub that's been shut down at short notice. What do you think? I've got gallons of the stuff."

"Good. There is just one thing, though. I lost my wallet so I can't pay."

"Don't worry about it," said Kent. "What use is money to us now anyway?"

"Fair point," said Andy. "Best you pour me a pint, then. Are you having one yourself?"

"I may as well," said Kent. "Though, perhaps we ought to be thinking about getting out of here while we still can."

"Why the fuck would we want to get out of here? Out there it is mayhem. In here we've got all the booze we could ever want. I suggest we stay safely holed up here for the duration."

"You think we're safe? I don't."

"Maybe not, but after a few pints we won't care, eh? And if the beer doesn't wash our troubles away then we can start on the spirits. I see the optics are well stocked."

"Come on then," said Kent, pouring two pints. This felt wrong somehow as if they were just giving up by sitting around and getting drunk. Fiddling while Rome burns came to mind. But he had to admit, Andy had been right. It wasn't going to be any safer outside and that opinion was being regularly reinforced by the frequent sounds of unrest coming from the street outside.

"Where have you been for the last few days, anyway? I thought you'd have been trying to bash the door down long before now, desperate to get back in?"

"Ah, well that's where I got lucky," said Andy. "I was on my way back down here on Tuesday to see if you'd let me in, when I walked past that posh wine shop, just up the road. You know, the one where all the London commuters who think they are too posh for the pub get their expensive wines to impress their dinner party friends?"

"Yes, but I've never been in it."

"Nor me, until this week. Anyway, as I walked past I noticed someone had kicked the door in. So I went in, and probably half the stock was gone. However, I did manage to procure for myself a couple of bottles of very expensive vintage malt whisky. So I grabbed hold of them and skedaddled off home."

"Which is where you've been ever since?"

"Correct. However, by this morning, I had finished them. So I thought I'd pop down and see if there was any more. But the whole shop's been almost cleaned out. The only thing left was a few bottles of some rosé wine and I don't like that. So that's when I thought of you."

"I'm touched," said Kent sarcastically. "So what's it like out there?"

"Horrible," said Andy.

"I wonder if they are saying anything on the television about it," said Kent. "They weren't yesterday. I think there must be some sort of news blackout."

He grabbed the remote from behind the bar and turned the television on to see if they could get any further information but every channel was broadcasting reruns of old material. On entertainment stations, it was home makeover or cookery shows, while on Sky Sports it was just footage of old football matches and documentaries. On the news channel, there was an endless loop showing the weather and out-of-date stock market prices, with elevator music over the top of it.

He switched it off in frustration, prompting Andy to suggest putting some songs on the jukebox instead. Surprisingly, after a few beers and a few classic tracks from the 1970s to the 1990s, the two men found themselves getting on quite well. After years of antagonistic conversations, now all they had left was each other they were finding kinship in the face of adversity. By the time it started to get dark, they were both quite enjoying themselves.

"What do you reckon was the best year ever for music?" asked Andy.

"Ooh, that's a tough one," said Kent, pausing to gather his thoughts. "I reckon maybe 1996. I was twenty years old and Britpop was all the rage. For once, the charts were filled up with music I liked."

"Oh, no, that's far too late," said Andy. "It was all way too commercial by then."

"It was always commercial," said Kent. "Look at Elvis and The Beatles, both marketing men's dreams."

"Yeah, but the nineties? All those girl and boy bands and who were that bloody pair of actors who kept doing cheesy cover versions of old songs for the grannies to buy?"

"Robson and Jerome?"

"That's them. And all that bloody dance music that all sounded the same."

"What's your best year, then, if mine's so bad?"

"1979," said Andy, confidently. "Brilliant year. You had all the post-punk bands, two-tone was kicking off and the start of heavy metal. What's not to like?"

"You can barely have been born in 1979," said Kent.

"Yes, but that doesn't stop me from appreciating the music of the era, does it? Lots of people enjoy listening to Beethoven but they weren't around in the nineteenth century."

"Fair enough. OK then, how about we have a competition? I'll put three songs from 1996 on the jukebox and you choose three from 1979. Then we'll decide whose is best. Whoever wins gets to choose which bottle of vintage malt we crack open from the top shelf."

"You're on," said Andy. "I'll go first." He headed over to the jukebox, and seconds later, the sound of The Jam began blaring out performing 'Eton Rifles'.

"Turn it up a bit," said Andy. "Let's rock!" he added, before starting what would have been an embarrassing display of air guitar had there been a full pub of people there to witness it.

"I'm not turning it up," said Kent. "The last thing we want to do is attract unwarranted attention."

The argument was rendered academic at that point because suddenly the jukebox went off and the pub was plummeted into semi-darkness.

"Bloody hell, I was enjoying that," said Andy. "What a time to get a power cut."

"I'll have to light some candles," said Kent. "It's gone half nine. It will be pitch dark soon. There are plenty on the tables in the restaurant. I'll just nip through and get some."

"The electricity won't be off that long, will it?" asked Andy, on his return. "They'll be working on it."

"Who is left to work on it?" said Kent, as he lit the candles, which Debs had stuck in the top of old wine bottles. "I'd put money on it not coming back on at all."

"No more music, then," said Andy, mournfully. "But at least we've still got the drink."

They didn't have it for long. The power was the last thing holding the remaining shreds of society together, and without it, the intermittent incidents out in the main street became one great free-for-all of raiding, looting, and fighting. Without CCTV, streetlights, or anything else to deter them, it was open season for the growing gangs.

Kent had done his best to fortify the front of the building by piling up furniture in front of the doors and windows but it was to no avail. Soon there was a hammering at the front door and the windows were being put through.

"What do we do now?" asked Andy, who despite the anaesthetising effect of all the alcohol was looking rather frightened as the reality of what was happening began to sink in."

"What can we do?" said Kent.

"Hide? Upstairs, maybe? And take a few bottles up?"

"What's the point? We're only delaying the inevitable."

"We could escape the back way. Through the gate."

"Too late," said Kent, as three men dressed in British Army outfits burst through the rear door. They must have come through the very gate which Andy had just mentioned.

"Stay where you are," said the lead man, who Kent was horrified to see was carrying a sawn-off shotgun. Where the hell had he got that from?

"How dare you come in here," said Kent, trying to bluster it out. "This is private property."

"Not anymore it isn't," said the man. "We're requisitioning this place. Government orders."

"Really?" asked Kent, peering closely at the man's uniform through the dim candle-lit room. "And what's your rank?"

"Lieutenant General," he replied. "And you are now under my command."

"Hmmm, then could you explain to me why you are wearing a captain's outfit?" asked Kent, who knew a fair bit about the military. "And not a current one either, but one from the 1940s? You know, if I didn't suspect better, I would say you had appropriated it from somewhere."

"He has!" said Andy. "I've seen it before. It came from the fancy dress shop on North Street. Nobby wore it for that VE Day anniversary party we had a few years ago."

"You're not real military at all, are you?" asked Kent of the man who was looking angry at being exposed as a fake.

"I bet that gun's not real either," added Andy.

"Oh, it's real alright," said the man, turning and aiming it above the bar and letting off a single shot where it shattered an unopened bottle of malt whisky into thousands of tiny pieces.

"What sort of animal are you?" exclaimed a horrified Andy. "That was a vintage bottle of Laphroaig!"

"Right, I've had enough of this," said the bogus officer. "It doesn't matter who or what I am, the fact is I've got the gun and we're taking over. Now you have two choices. You can make an issue of it and get yourselves shot. Or you can piss off out of my sight within the next sixty seconds and take your chances outside."

"Come on, Andy, it isn't really a choice at all when he puts it like that, is it?" said a resigned Kent.

144

"Can I take a bottle of scotch with me for the road?" asked Andy hopefully. "I can still see some Glenfiddich up there."

"No, you cannot. Everything in here belongs to us now. You've got fifty seconds left before I blow your brains out."

"We're going," said Kent, propelling Andy out through the back door and towards the gate which had been smashed off its hinges.

"I didn't even have time for a wee," protested Andy. "I never leave the pub without having a wee first."

"Do it out here, then," said Kent. "I'm sure it won't be the first time."

"Very well," said Andy, unzipping his ancient jeans and aiming up against a lamppost.

As Kent looked the other way, listening to Andy urinating combined with the growing sounds of rioting all around him, he had to admit that events had taken a seriously depressing turn.

Chapter Ten
July 2023

At Hannah's house, the following morning, the five temporary occupants were still debating the best course of action.

The failure of the electricity supply during the previous evening had forced their hand. Most of them were in favour of leaving today, but they still couldn't agree on the details.

"That's the last of the milk," said Kaylee, as she passed it to Lauren to pour on her cereal.

"No coffee, then," replied Lauren, already knowing what the answer would be.

"Unless you're planning to start a fire in the back garden and boil a pan of water over it, no," said Josh.

"Everything else in this fridge needs to be eaten today," said Kaylee. "It's already getting warm. And the freezer is starting to defrost."

"I hadn't even thought about the implications of the power going off," said Charlie. "Just think of all those freezers, all over the country, full of food that is going to thaw out and rot."

"And it's not as if we can even cook any of this stuff," said Josh, rummaging around in the freezer and pulling out packs of frozen chicken and pizzas.

"We could have a barbecue," suggested Lauren, who was the only one who had been in favour of staying longer at the house during the previous evening's discussions.

"And attract every hungry person in the neighbourhood?" replied Josh. "I don't think so."

"So we can't cook anything," said Seema. "We can't preserve anything. What does that leave us with?"

"Tins, bottles, long-life food. Anything that doesn't need to be kept cool," said Josh.

"And how much of that stuff do we have?" asked Seema.

"Not a lot to be honest," said Lauren, who had been staying at the house the longest and had eaten her way through most of the food that Hannah had left behind.

"And what about your mother's supplies?"

"Oh, she's stocked up to the ceiling. Literally, in the case of my bedroom. But like I said, I can't see her being willing to share it with me, let alone all of you."

"I still think you should try and persuade her. I don't like the idea of us heading out into the unknown without adequate provisions," said Josh.

"I don't see why we have to leave at all," said Lauren. "There must be plenty of food still out there. I mean, with all the disappearances, there won't be that many people left to eat it. Yes, I know we've no power, but it's summer. We won't freeze."

"There are still plenty of people around who will be scavenging for what they can find. You've been holed up in here all week and you haven't seen how bad things have got out there. I have," replied Josh.

"All the more reason to stay here then," said Lauren. "You may think it's worth the risk of getting raped or murdered for a tin of beans but I don't. Wouldn't we be better off checking the houses in this street first to see if any are empty? We could do it after dark when we won't be seen. One of them could have a stock of food that could last us for weeks."

"It's not just about the food we can store," said Josh. "There are other considerations. What about all the stuff that's going to go rotten, not just here but in the other houses? There is no one to collect the bins so it will be a magnet for flies and vermin. And with that comes diseases. And what about water? We've lost electricity and gas. How do we know what comes out of the tap is safe? And how do we flush the toilet if we lose the supply altogether?"

"Water isn't powered by electricity, though, is it?" asked Lauren. "It's all mechanical, through pipes."

"I don't know exactly," admitted Josh. "But I'm sure it must go through some sort of mechanical purification process before it's put into the supply. It's not going to keep flowing safely forever."

"But what makes you think going out in the country is going to be any better? There will be fewer facilities there, not more."

"We can find the things we need out there," said Charlie. "It will be like going camping. We just need to find a supply of fresh water, and things we can safely eat and drink in the wild."

"I hate the countryside," said Lauren. "It's full of bugs and stinging nettles and cowpats. Not my idea of fun."

"You know I'm surprised at you, Lauren," said Kaylee. "You're normally the adventurous one."

"I'm a lot more adventurous than you, in every way. But this idea of going and living off the land sounds insane. I mean, none of you are exactly Bear Grylls, are you? I don't think you would have a clue what to do out there."

"Josh and I used to be in the scouts," said Charlie. "They teach you this sort of stuff."

"Like what?" asked Lauren.

"How to start a fire rubbing sticks together, tie knots, that sort of thing."

"Very useful," said Lauren sarcastically. "And what about food? Do they teach you in the scouts how to hunt? Do you know which mushrooms are safe to eat and which are going to lead to an agonising and painful death as they dissolve your internal organs? I don't think you've got a clue about any of these things. I think you've just come up with some fanciful idea about getting back to nature and living off the land which is just a complete fantasy."

"I have to say, she's got a point," said Seema. "It all sounds very romantic and adventurous but in reality, it's not going to be a lot of fun at all."

"Thank you," said Lauren, grateful for her support.

"However, I still don't think we can stay here, for the reasons Josh gave," added Seema. "But it would be crazy to go off into the country ill-equipped. I mean, when people go camping, they don't have to go foraging for mushrooms. They take everything they need with them. If we can get hold of a reasonable supply of food, a gas-powered stove, lots of bottled water, toilet paper and everything else we might need, then it's feasible."

"And a tent?" asked Lauren.

"Not necessarily," said Seema. "There must be some remote cottages that are empty by now. The thing is, though, how are we going to carry all this stuff? There won't be much room in my Kia, with all five of us in it."

"We need a van," said Josh. "My dad's a builder. He's got one. Except, I can't drive. But you can. And so can Charlie."

"Even better, why don't we find a camper van or mobile home that's already kitted out for this sort of thing?" suggested Charlie. "You mentioned before that's what your parents have done."

"More by luck than judgement," said Josh. "They didn't know all this was coming."

"I think that's an excellent idea," said Seema. "People take them to festivals all the time. They've got stoves, sinks, even toilet facilities."

"Now this is beginning to sound more feasible," said Lauren. "Rather than rushing off unprepared."

"Yes, assuming we can find such a suitably equipped vehicle with a full tank of petrol," said Charlie. "Because none of the petrol stations will be open."

"We should try Murray's," suggested Josh. "That's where my dad got his from."

"Will it have everything we need?" asked Lauren.

"I doubt we'll be that lucky," said Josh. "Doug Murray specialises in cheap holiday hires, not great big millionaire motorhomes."

"So what about all the other stuff we need?" asked Lauren.

"We go out and find it," said Charlie. "That's what we do with the rest of today and tonight. Go out, get what we need then meet back here."

"And if we encounter other people with the same idea?" asked Kaylee. "They might not be as friendly as we are."

"Then we go prepared," said Josh, reaching for a knife block on the kitchen counter and taking out a hefty carving knife, which he then brandished in front of him.

151

"You're not serious," said Kaylee, shocked at what Josh seemed to be suggesting.

"Look, Kaylee, don't take this the wrong way, but you can be a bit of a wet blanket at times. If you had seen what I saw yesterday, you would know that you need to protect yourself out there."

"By stabbing people?"

"I'm not planning on stabbing anyone. It's just a deterrent. In case things turn nasty."

"I'm sure that's what all those young men out on the streets of London say when they go out carrying knives. And how many of them get knifed to death every year?"

"This is a completely different situation, Kaylee," said Josh. "I'm not talking about going for a stroll around Regent's Park, tooled up. If we don't protect ourselves, we have a very real chance of ending up dead."

"I'm sorry to say it, but he's right," said Seema, lifting a jug on the kitchen table and pouring herself some orange juice. "Does anyone want the last of this?"

"Please," said Kaylee.

"You see, that's all the milk gone, and all the orange juice," said Josh. "Now we have no choice – we need to leave. I wanted to go today, but I get what everyone's saying. We need to prepare more. So let's spend today doing that, and then leave before first light tomorrow morning, when hopefully there won't be many people around."

"OK, you've persuaded me," said Lauren. "Let's start drawing up a list."

Two men who had set out the previous night with no plan or list were Kent and Andy. They had endured a fraught journey out of the town, not helped by them both being drunk. Despite their lack of preparedness, they still had the right idea, which was to get out into the country. They encountered a few threatening people on the way, but when it became apparent they had nothing of value on them, they were left alone.

By midnight, they were out in the country and walking, or rather staggering, along a footpath that led towards a village, about three miles away. Guided only by moonlight, they had gone about halfway when they had to get over a stile, at which point Andy fell into a pile of stinging nettles and Kent had to drag him out. Once they were back on their feet, Kent spotted a barn about a hundred yards away from the footpath. Deciding it might provide suitable shelter for the night, they stumbled over a ploughed field towards it, before collapsing onto the bales of hay inside.

Some hours later, a hungover Kent awoke to feel something wet and warm nuzzling his face.

"What the fuck!" he exclaimed, squinting to focus his bleary eyes in the face of the sunbeams that were streaming between gaps in the wooden slats of the ageing barn. He jumped up, startling the horse that had been curiously probing his face.

"Get up!" he said, poking a snoring Andy in the ribs with his foot, causing him to sit up in a similarly beleaguered state.

"What's going on?" said Andy. "Where are we?"

In his drunken stupor, he hadn't retained any short-term memories of their arrival here in the middle of the night.

"In a barn," said Kent, looking around him.

"Why?" said Andy, trying to piece together what fragments from earlier in the previous evening he could remember. "And what's that slobber all over your face?"

"It was that bloody horse, dribbling all over me," said Kent, pointing at the animal that had now gone over to drink from a trough at the other end of the barn.

"Bad luck," said Andy.

"It could have been worse," said Kent. "For one horrible moment, I thought it was you."

"I'm not that desperate yet," said Andy. "It's not like we're the last two people on Earth, is it? You're safe for now."

"I sincerely hope that is a joke," said Kent.

"Shame there are no chickens in here," said Andy. "I could just do with a couple of eggs."

"And how would you cook them?" asked Kent.

"Good point," said Andy. "Perhaps we had better go and look for some breakfast."

"Like what?" asked Kent. "Dandelion tea? Bark muesli? Stinging nettles on toast?"

"This is a farm, isn't it? Perhaps the farmer will have some food."

"And he'll be happy to share it with us, will he?"

"Well, no harm in asking," said Andy.

They didn't get as far as asking. When they stepped out of the barn, they could see the farmhouse up ahead and began to make their way towards it via a track that ran alongside a field of corn.

"You know, this place seems familiar," said Kent, just before the sound of a shotgun rang out and a bullet whistled past and embedded itself in the wall of the barn behind them.

"Jesus Christ!" exclaimed Andy.

"So much for no harm in asking," said Kent, as they turned and ran back towards the barn.

"Cattle rustlers," a voice bellowed behind them. "I'll have you this time, you see if I don't."

They reached the barn just as another shot hit the wall, causing the horse inside to neigh and rear up. Their hurried entrance did little to calm it.

"That horse looks cross," said Andy.

155

"Just don't get behind it," said Kent. "You don't want to get kicked, it could be very nasty."

They dove behind the same hay bales they had slept on but they weren't safe yet. The farmer had seen them enter and was now bearing down on the barn, determined to catch them.

"Come on, I know you're in there," he shouted, as the creaky barn door swung open.

"Wait a moment, I know that voice," said Kent, taking a chance and leaping upwards.

"Don't shoot, Mr Tuddenham, it's me, Richard Kent. Remember?"

"Kent? DI Richard Kent?" asked Arthur, instantly relaxing his tone. "Of course, I remember you! You helped me get my tractor back after those bloody yobs stole it."

"You mean he actually solved a crime?" asked Andy in amazement, getting to his feet.

"Oh, yes, DI Kent here was the best we ever had. Much better than that useless woman that's in charge now."

"Well, one does one's best," said Kent, revelling in this rare and probably undeserved moment of praise.

"What brings you here, then, Richard? Have you come to help me solve the riddle of my missing cattle? You're just the man I need on the case! That lot down at the station aren't interested."

"Umm, yes, that's right," said Kent, recognising that getting on Arthur's good side would be a very sensible thing to do. "Hannah's very busy so she's called me back on a consultancy basis."

"Eh?" said Andy, not so quick on the uptake.

"Sort of like a private detective, is that what you mean?" asked Arthur.

"Yes, that's it," said Kent. "I'd give you one of my cards but I've been so popular as an amateur sleuth that I've run out!"

"And who is this you have with you?" asked Arthur looking at Kent's scruffy companion with disdain.

"Oh, this is my assistant, Andy. Think of him as a sort of Watson to my Holmes. Plain clothes, obviously."

"Very plain," remarked Arthur, not impressed by Andy's faded and dirty denim. "He doesn't exactly look the part, does he?"

"Ah, well that's the beauty of it," said Kent. "To lull the villains into a false sense of security. They would never believe that anyone dressed like him could possibly have an ounce of intelligence. Though I have to say, he's perfectly dressed for this job. Looks like a proper farm hand."

"Yes, he should blend in nicely," said Arthur. "But I'm confused. You could have just driven up to the farm. Why have you been hiding out in the barn all night?"

157

"Ah, well, police records on this sort of thing show that cattle rustlers mostly strike at night. We thought we would camp out here and try and catch them. As it happens, Arthur, we might need to stay a few days, if maybe you could put us up?"

"Yes," said Andy, who had now worked out where Kent was going with all this. "It's a very complex operation. Needs very careful planning."

"It might be better if we stayed in the house, though, and kept watch from there. The barn is a little uncomfortable," said Kent.

"Oh, yes, DI Kent, that will be no problem at all. However, I think if you're really going to convince these villains that you are bona fide farm workers, you might have to help me out during the day a little. You see, Caleb, that's my main farm hand, hasn't turned up for the past few days and there is a lot to do. It's coming up to harvest time."

"What, you mean work?" exclaimed a perturbed Andy.

"Yes, Andy, work," said Kent. "You remember; that thing you used to do for your beer money before you conned the social into believing you had a disability?"

"I can't pay you, but there's bed and board thrown in," said Arthur.

"Wait a moment!" said Andy, who had spotted some glass jars on the other side of the barn. He wandered over to examine them and was delighted by what he saw.

"Hey, Kent! There's a stash of cider over here!"

"Oh, and as much cider as you can drink," said Arthur. "It's a sideline I started up a couple of years ago. It sells like hot cakes in my neighbour's farm shop."

"When do we start?" asked a newly eager Andy, now he knew that alcohol was involved.

"Today. Do either of you know how to drive a tractor?"

"How hard can it be?" asked Andy.

"That's the spirit," said Arthur.

"There is one thing," said Kent.

"Just name it, my good man," said Arthur.

"Could we have some breakfast?"

"Of course, come over to the farmhouse. My hens have laid a good crop of eggs this morning."

"How are you going to cook them?" asked Andy. "Hasn't your electricity gone off?"

"Oh, you've had the power cuts too, have you? Yes, went off last night, but don't you worry about that, my lad. Come and see."

As Kent stepped into the old-fashioned farmhouse kitchen, he felt as if he had been transported back in time. The room was reminiscent of a bygone era as the sunlight filtered through the small weathered windows, casting gentle shadows on the tarnished wooden floors.

In the heart of the kitchen stood a majestic wood-burning stove. It looked ancient, but there was no doubting the durability of its cast-iron frame and Kent could feel the heat coming from it as soon as he stepped into the room. In a world devoid of electricity and gas, it was worth its weight in gold.

Looking around, he could see many shelves, filled with an array of earthenware and stoneware dishes. They also held jars of preserved fruits and vegetables, a testament to Arthur's old-fashioned self-sufficiency. In one corner, there was even a traditional butter churn, one of several anachronistic devices in the room that had long fallen out of daily usage in the wider world but could come in very handy, given the current circumstances.

If they were to live out their days in a post-apocalyptic environment, there could not have been many better places to end up in than this. If it meant putting in a few hours' work on the farm to stay here, it would be well worth it.

After a welcome breakfast of eggs and bacon, cooked on the ancient, blackened stove which was powered by wood alone, Kent and Andy had shaken off their hangovers and felt ready to face the day.

Chapter Eleven
July 2023

At long last, following countless hours of detailed discussions around the kitchen table, Lauren and the others had forged a rough survival plan to see them through the next couple of days.

They didn't want to leave the house undefended, so left Kaylee on guard duty with strict instructions not to open the door to anyone, while the others split into two pairs. Charlie had initially been against this, as he felt that she would be vulnerable left alone. But five was an odd number, and as Josh pointed out, being in the house by herself would still be safer than being outside in a world that now had all the lawlessness of the Wild West.

Josh had suggested that the remaining four of them should go out in mixed-sex pairings so that each woman would have a man with her for protection. That did not go down well, sparking outrage from both Lauren and Seema who denounced his outdated, patriarchal stance. Besides, having hit it off so well, they were keen to work together, so Seema suggested they team up to acquire food for the journey that lay ahead. Their first stop was Lauren's family home to see if they could persuade Patricia to part with some of her stockpile. Lauren wasn't optimistic they would be successful, but knowing how much she had stacked away, they had to try.

They travelled the short distance there in Seema's Kia, which was risky as it would have been easier to keep out of sight on foot. But they knew that if they walked they would not have been able to carry very much and would be more vulnerable to attack. At least the electric car was able to cruise along without making too much noise.

"We won't be able to use this car again after today," said Seema, glancing at the dashboard. "I've got about thirty miles left, and with the electricity off, this car will be useless once the battery's dead. And it's too small for all five of us, anyway. We wouldn't be able to take hardly anything with us."

"Let's hope the boys find something bigger," said Lauren, referring to Charlie and Josh's prime mission for the day.

"There doesn't seem to be anyone much about," said Seema.

"No," replied Lauren, casting her eyes from side to side as they moved slowly through the residential streets. "That surprises me."

"Perhaps they are afraid to set foot outside, and who can blame them? Did you hear that woman screaming in the night? I still feel bad we didn't go out to investigate. But then what could we have done?"

"Befallen the same fate as her and drawn attention to ourselves, no doubt. But we can't hide away forever. At some point, we're going to face a fight. Turn right at the end here."

"That's why we need to be prepared," said Seema. "It's a shame your friend Hannah isn't still around. She's a senior

162

police officer. She might have known where we could get our hands on some proper weapons."

"Do you know her?"

"Yes, I've interviewed her on the news a couple of times. I like her. Honest, gutsy, and good at her job. You can't say that about many people these days."

"You must have met a lot of famous people."

"Not really. It's the national stations that get all the glamour."

"Well, you're famous around here. It feels surreal sitting here with you. I've often wondered how odd it must be to be a celebrity. Everyone knows who you are, but you don't know who they are."

"I'm hardly a celebrity. I'm a local news reporter."

"Well, I feel like I know you. Like I've always known you. Does that sound odd?"

"No, not really. The feeling's mutual. You know how sometimes you meet someone, and you feel like you've known them all your life? Or maybe you were friends in a previous life? That's what this feels like. It's a bit like déjà vu but with a person rather than a situation."

"I feel like that too. It's as if fate brought us together," said Lauren. "Take the next left."

"Well, let's hope it doesn't end up being a grisly fate," said Seema. "I feel incredibly apprehensive driving around like this as if we're going to get attacked at any moment."

"As I said, we must face facts – sooner or later we're going to have to fight, possibly for our lives. One thing I've never done in my life is shy away from a fight if it's standing up for something I believe in, or to protect someone I care about."

"I can tell that, just from the short time I've known you. Honest and gutsy – they're qualities I can see in you too."

"Well, so far today, fate seems to be on our side. I'm surprised we've got this far without being accosted, but I'm not complaining. I don't want to have to use this, but I am not afraid to if I have to."

She showed Seema the kitchen knife that Josh had given her before they left.

"Let's hope our luck holds," replied Seema, not relishing the prospect of a bloody battle.

Their luck did hold and soon they were parking up outside Patricia's house. The curtains were drawn tight, and there was no sound from within, so Lauren decided to let herself in with her key rather than knocking. She and Seema crept into the hallway, trying not to be heard but that wasn't going to be easy. With the electricity off, there was no television or any other background noise to cover the sound of the door opening or their footsteps.

"I'm not sure if she's even here," said Lauren.

"Perhaps she went to the Rapture," suggested Seema.

"Is that what we're calling it now? There's a guy in the main street who keeps banging on about that, assuming he's still around. But I don't believe it for a second. I can sort of understand why people who are into religion might, but that's not my thing."

"It's just a phrase that's sort of stuck, I suppose. We get this a lot in journalism. Someone coins a phrase, something like Brexit or Partygate, and within a couple of days, every newspaper has adopted it. We need a name for this so we've christened it the Rapture, whether we believe in God or not."

But Patricia hadn't gone to the Rapture. As Seema finished speaking, the kitchen door was thrown open to reveal her, brandishing a crossbow which was aimed squarely at them.

"What the hell is that thing?" said Lauren. "Put it down, Mother, before you kill someone. It's me!"

Slowly, Patricia lowered the weapon, eyeing them both with suspicion.

"I got it for defence," she said. "I've already seen off one thief who tried to get in here. He won't be back."

"Is that thing even legal?" asked Seema.

"What's it got to do with you?" said Patricia angrily.

"Don't be so rude, Mum. This is Seema. She's a friend."

"I know exactly who she is. You work for the BBC, don't you?"

"I do."

"Well, I don't trust the BBC. Which means I don't trust you. Now what are you two doing here?"

"I didn't realise I now needed permission to enter my family home," said Lauren.

"No one gets in here without my say-so. I've been preparing a long time for this day and nobody is going to take this moment away from me. People laughed at me and said I was some sort of conspiracy theorist. Not laughing anymore, are they?"

"Yes, regarding your prepping, we were wondering if you might be able to spare us a bit of food. You've got plenty."

"Why should I? You were one of the worst. Mocking me and calling me a nutter. Do you still think I'm crazy now?"

"No, I don't," said Lauren, thinking that a little false flattery might do the trick. But it didn't work.

"Don't try and sweet talk me. It's too late for that. If you want any of the food here, you need to stay here and help me defend it. Then I'll share it with you. But not her. She can get out, right now."

She raised the crossbow again slightly and pointed it threateningly in Seema's direction.

"You would send her back out there, alone? She nearly got raped yesterday."

"That's not my problem. She's not welcome here. Now are you staying or not?"

"Not. But please, can't you just let us take a few tins? You've got thousands up there."

"And I need them all. It's your fault for not preparing. Ever heard the story of the ant and the grasshopper?"

"Funnily enough, no. From what I recall there weren't a lot of bedtime stories when I was little. You were always too busy."

"Well I'm the ant and you're the grasshopper. While you were busy getting drunk and shagging about, I was preparing for what was coming. Now you'll reap the consequences."

"You really don't care about me at all, do you?" asked Lauren.

Patricia paused for a bit, contemplating her answer.

"No, quite honestly, I don't. Having you was the worst mistake of my life. I should have had an abortion when I had the chance. Now get out, both of you."

"Fine," said Lauren, biting her lip as she struggled to process the sheer level of spite of her mother's last statement. "But before I do, I'm going up those stairs and I'm going to take whatever I can carry. And if you want to stop me, you are going

167

to have to shoot me. I don't believe even you are capable of that. Then, when I'm gone, you won't see me again. Ever."

With that, she turned and ascended the stairs, as Patricia swiftly trained the crossbow on her back. Lauren was taking a big gamble, and felt giddy with fear, wondering with every step if she was going to feel a projectile embedded in her back. She knew she was endangering Seema too, but thought back to their discussion in the car about needing to fight for their lives. Making a stand here was the first part of that process. What she couldn't believe was that it was against her own flesh and blood.

Could she kill her mother if she had to? In some ways, she was glad she had left the knife in the car, out of harm's way. She hadn't expected to need it in here, but the way things were going, she was beginning to regret that decision.

There were thousands of cans of food upstairs, even more than the last time she had been there. Her mother had been stocking up. She took two six-packs of baked beans and four five-packs of tuna. It wasn't a lot, but it was a start, and this was more about making a point than anything else.

Cradling the food in her arms she headed back downstairs to find her mother shaking with what to Lauren looked like a mix of fear and anger. She looked decidedly unhinged which, given that the crossbow was now pointed directly at Seema, was an incredibly dangerous situation. She just hoped that, in her agitated state, she wasn't going to discharge the crossbow accidentally.

168

"Put that food down or I'll kill her," she said, her voice full of aggression, but Lauren knew it was an empty threat.

"Don't do it, Lauren," said Seema. "We need that food."

"I'm not going to do it," she replied. "She doesn't have the guts."

"Try me," said Patricia.

"We will. Can you open the door for me, Seema? My hands are rather full."

Seema obliged, opening the front door and leading Lauren outside, after which she slammed it shut. As she did, they heard the thud of a crossbow bolt embedding itself in the door behind them. It was true, she hadn't had the guts. That shot had been fired in anger once it could no longer harm them.

Lauren could scarcely believe how courageous she had been, but once they were a few yards beyond the front door, the sheer enormity of the experience she had just been through hit her and she burst into tears, dropping one of her packs of tuna in the process.

It was so unlike her. Normally, so tough, so self-assured, she couldn't remember the last time she had cried. But this time she just let it all out.

"It's OK," said Seema, taking Lauren in her arms and giving her a comforting hug. "She doesn't deserve you. And you don't need her anymore. You just proved that. You were incredibly brave, and I'm so proud of you!"

169

Lauren took great comfort from Seema's support and knew that what she was saying was true.

"You're right," she said, as the sobs began to subside. "Let her rot away in the prison of her own making. At least we're trying to do something."

"That's the spirit," said Seema. "Now, let's get this lot into the car and go and see what else we can find."

Elsewhere, Josh and Charlie had gone on foot, first to Charlie's house, as Kaylee had been insistent that they check on their parents. When they got there, Charlie was in for a shock. There hadn't seemed to be anyone around at first. However, when Charlie went upstairs, Phil emerged from Sarah's bedroom, wearing one of his mother's dressing gowns.

Despite their protestations, it was obvious what had been going on, even more so when they expressed no interest in joining the others on their journey to find a safer place in the country.

Their next stop was three miles away, at a specialist camper and motorhome hire centre, based on the outskirts of one of the neighbouring villages. This necessitated acquiring a couple of bicycles to make the trip, but this didn't prove difficult. Josh thought that they might have to take them from a shop as he had back in Oxford, but when they walked into town they discovered that there were several abandoned ones just lying around waiting to be taken.

They had a couple of worrying moments, most notably when encountering a man staggering around waving a broken bottle but it quickly became clear that he was blind drunk. They easily dodged him, leaving him swearing incoherently behind them.

They saw few other people on the journey, leading them to draw the same conclusion as Seema and Lauren. People had become too frightened to leave their homes. To maximise their chances of staying out of sight, they chose their route to the nearby village carefully. Having grown up in the area they knew every inch of footpath and bridleway for miles around, and wisely used these rather than the roads. It was safer but challenging, and they had to carry the bikes over a couple of stiles, as well as avoiding the nettles and thistles which were thriving after the wet summer and swamping some of the paths.

Doug Murray's motorhome and campervan hire business had seen better days. The tarmac, which housed the dozen or so vehicles he hired out, was crumbling and being encroached on by weeds. The vehicles themselves were also hardly in mint condition, but they were exactly what Josh and Charlie were looking for. All they needed to do now was gain access to one with enough petrol to get them where they needed to go.

The showroom was closed, like everything else. They got off their bikes, propped them up against a wall and tried the doors of the various vehicles. All were locked.

"What do we do now?" asked Charlie.

"The keys will be in the showroom. We need to get inside."

"How? Smash the window?"

"That's what I was thinking. I'm amazed someone else hasn't had the same idea and done it already."

"Seems a bit drastic. Perhaps we should try knocking on the door first," said Charlie.

"Alright, but I doubt anyone will answer."

To Charlie's satisfaction, his know-it-all friend was wrong for once. After a few solid thumps on the door, they heard a voice coming from somewhere inside.

"We're closed. Go away."

"Mr Murray, is that you?" asked Josh. "My name's Josh Gardner. You hired a campervan out to my dad last week."

"Geoff Gardner?"

"That's him."

"Hold on a minute," came the reply, and then Doug Murray appeared, complete with a set of keys to open the glass door. He was a slight, bespectacled man in his fifties and was going grey. It had been years since Josh had last seen him, and he looked as though he had aged a lot.

"So you're Geoff's boy, eh?" he said, looking him up and down. "My, my, you've grown! Last time I saw you, you were knee-high to a grasshopper."

"I used to come here as a kid," explained Josh to Charlie.

"He did, and he loved it!" said Doug. "I used to put him up in one of the cabs so he could pretend he could drive it, and he used to make all the engine noises, and gear changes, didn't you?"

"Ah, how sweet," said Charlie, enjoying Josh's embarrassment at having these childhood revelations brought up.

"So what can I do for you, my boy?" asked Doug. "There's not a problem with the campervan, is there?"

"Oh, no, it's fine," said Josh. "It's just that, we were kind of hoping you could let us have one?"

"Of course," said Doug. "Me and your dad go way back. We were at school together. And he did a marvellous job building my extension. You've not thought of joining the family business yourself, though, so Geoff tells me."

"No, that's more my brother's thing. I decided to go to university instead."

"There's nothing wrong with getting a decent education," said Doug. "But listen, about you having one of these vehicles. Are you sure that's a good idea? I mean, there are some very strange things going on as I'm sure you know. It could be dangerous out there."

"That's why we want it," replied Josh. "There are five of us and it's not safe to stay in the town. We want to get out into the countryside and try and be self-sufficient for a while. We thought a motorhome might be the perfect solution – what with the power being off and everything."

"Yes, I can see that," said Doug. "But it's not something I would want to do myself. I think I'll be better off here. There is only me, after all, and we haven't had any trouble in the village so far. Now, let's see what we can find."

He went back inside and emerged again a minute or two later with some more keys.

"Yes, this is the one you want, it's designed for six," he said, leading them over to the largest vehicle on the site. It was a good deal taller and wider than a VW campervan and of a considerably sturdier design. It was light blue and had windows along the entire length, though these were currently shielded by blackout curtains for privacy.

"Allow me to present the SuperDeluxe 2000!" he announced.

"Why is it called the 2000?" said Charlie.

"Because that's the year it was built, going by the number plate," said Josh, noting that it ended with an X, and also that there were signs of rust around the wheel arches. Still, not to worry. They were borrowing it, not buying it.

"OK, it's a vintage model, but it's still a classic," said Doug. "Here, why don't you take a look inside?"

He opened the rear doors and they looked into the van, approving of what they saw. The vehicle might have been old, but it was well equipped, as Doug explained as he went through his sales pitch.

"You see these benches down either side? These slide and convert into bunks at night. And it has a table, here, which folds out from the wall when you need it."

"Very handy," remarked Charlie. "What about the catering arrangements?"

"You've got a sink here, and a two-burner gas stove," said Doug. "There's also a fridge, but that's electric. It's got a battery for when you're on the move, but you need to hook up to the mains when you're parked up."

"That could be a problem," said Josh. "What about the bathroom facilities?" he asked, noticing a small sealed-off area.

"You've got a compact bathroom in there with a shower and a chemical toilet, but you need water. There's a tank, but it needs refilling."

"What about petrol?"

"It's got a full tank, all ready for hire. You'll get about four hundred miles out of it, but after that, I'm not sure where you'll find more."

"And you don't mind us taking this?" asked Josh. "I mean, we can't pay you, with the debit card systems being offline."

"Please, we can settle up later when all this blows over. Your dad has been a good friend to me over the years. It's the least I can do."

"Brilliant! We'll take it."

Doug couldn't have been more helpful, ensuring they had plenty of gas, a rechargeable battery, and fully stocked water tanks before Charlie drove the SuperDeluxe out of the car park and back onto the road.

"Now what?" asked Charlie.

"We get back to the others, and we get out of Dodge, as they used to say in the old Westerns. Tonight, or very early tomorrow morning. We can't leave this parked outside the house unattended. It's too risky."

"Agreed," replied Charlie, as they made their way back to town.

Chapter Twelve
August 2023

Andy and Kent were enjoying their time on the farm. It was hard work, but at least they were well fed and watered.

Andy had been spending his time driving up and down fields in the tractor, getting crops in and swigging cider as he went. Consequently, his lines were not particularly straight, but he had managed to gather a decent amount of grain. Unfortunately, after a couple of days, he used up the last of the farm's supply of diesel and had to stop.

Kent had been helping Arthur milk the dwindling supply of cows, a job that they had now resorted to doing by hand. It was long, hard work, and it became clear after a couple of days that none of the milk was ever going to be collected. They ended up consuming as much as they could themselves, as well as making cheese, another skill that Arthur possessed.

By now, Kent had managed to make Arthur understand what was happening in the outside world but the veteran farmer seemed unfazed. He had been brought up to learn every job on the farm back in the 1950s before technology had taken over. He seemed quite confident that they would be able to live off the fat of the land. With each new task, he imparted his years of experience to his new recruits, who were learning skills they hadn't ever contemplated needing in their comfortable existence in the old world.

On the day after the diesel ran out, a small pickup truck drove up the driveway, with a couple of young men visible inside. Arthur didn't even wait to find out who they were but began firing off bullets in their general direction. They soon got the message and turned around. After that, all was quiet.

In the evenings they would eat well. It went without saying that Arthur was a skilled butcher and every day they ate freshly killed food, often one of the many chickens that roamed the farmyard. Arthur had no end of other stored food too, pickles, preserves, and honey, as well as flour for making bread which they were able to bake in the wood-fired stove. It seemed there was nothing he couldn't do.

As apocalypses went, all things considered, it could be said that Kent and Andy were having a good one.

After dark, they drank around a fire which Arthur lit every night in the grand old fireplace in the living room, despite the warm weather. He lit it for the light, more than the heat. Gathered there, they talked and put the world to rights.

"It amazes me how much you manage to do around here," said Kent. "And all without a wife or family to help you."

"I've been doing it all my life," said Arthur. "And I don't need a woman fussing around after me."

"Not the marrying kind, eh?" said Andy.

"Well, I had my dalliances in my youth, like most men," said Arthur. "But I'm too set in my ways to compromise now."

178

"I could do with a woman," said Andy. "I mean, not to marry, just for a bit of company, if you know what I mean."

"Ha, you'll be lucky," said Kent. "All those years in the pub and I've never seen you pull ever."

"You should have seen me twenty years ago, mate, when I was famous. They were literally dripping off me."

"What a horrible thought," said Kent. "Looks like you'll just have to console yourself with your memories, then."

"I didn't know you were famous," said Arthur.

"For the proverbial fifteen minutes," said Kent. "And infamous would be a more accurate description."

"How about you, Richard? You must get your fair share of the ladies, running a pub," asked Arthur.

"You must be joking, he's way too old and fat," said Andy.

"Too old, too fat, and too married," said Kent. "And I'm perfectly fine with that."

"You may have given up on women, but I haven't," said Andy. "Listen, I've been thinking about it. All these people disappearing means this could be the best opportunity we've had to pull some birds for years."

"What do you mean?" said Kent. "That doesn't make sense. There are fewer women around now than there have ever been."

"Yeah, but there will be a lot less blokes too. What about all those women out there who have boyfriends and husbands that have disappeared? They'll be on their own now, and women have needs, just like we do. Think of it in marketing terms. There's a gap in the market which we could be filling."

"Andy, that's the worst idea I've ever heard," said Kent. "And there's not a marketing man alive who could make you a viable proposition."

"Ah, come on, it's worth a try, don't you think, Arthur?"

"Hmmm, and these women are going to just wander onto the farm, are they?" said Arthur.

"Yes, if you don't shoot them. Then we provide them with food and shelter and protection, and then we'll be heroes and they'll show their gratitude."

"Andy, you are talking utter bollocks," said Kent. "How strong is that cider you've been giving him?"

"About 9%," said Arthur.

"That would explain it. Perhaps we'd better give him some milk to sober up."

"We've got more than enough of it," said Arthur. "If we don't drink it we'll be pouring it away. We've no way to keep it cool."

"I don't want any bloody milk, that's a kid's drink," said Andy. "I want a woman. And in the morning, I'm going into town to find one."

"Comments like that make you sound like some sort of sex pest," said Kent. "I think you ought to go to bed and we'll talk about it in the morning."

But first thing the following day, Andy was gone.

"You don't really think he went into town looking for women, do you?" asked Arthur. "Now that the tractor's out of action I was hoping to get him to help us milk these cows."

"Is there much point?" said Kent, looking around the cowshed. "You've still got six of them. Surely we can get more than enough for our needs from just one?"

"It's really bad for a cow if it's not milked," said Arthur. "Imagine needing a piss and not being able to go. It can lead to all sorts of problems."

"Oh, right," said Kent, who was learning new things every day. "For the record, I don't think Andy has left. Well, not for town, anyway. I think he's gone to the Rapture, or been taken by the aliens, or whatever."

"Along with another of my cows," said Arthur. "There were seven here yesterday. I wonder what the aliens need them for."

"Maybe there's a shortage of milk on their planet," suggested Kent in a lame attempt at a joke, but Arthur didn't seem to realise that he was speaking in jest."

"Could be. Anyway, best we get started. There will be even more work for us to do now there are only two of us. It's not just the cows, there are crops to get in which is going to be a long job with no tractor. Plus, I need to sort out the drainage in the lower field."

"Great," said Kent half-heartedly. He had never done so much physical labour in all his life. The only positive thing he had to say about it was that he was shedding loads of weight.

Kent and Arthur had risen not long after dawn, but Josh and the others were already on the road by then. They had considered leaving the previous evening but there had been so much to do, it had already been dark by the time they had got the campervan loaded up.

It was relatively safe in the secluded lane behind Hannah's house, compared to the main streets. There, gangs of youths were roaming, fighting, and setting fire to things at night. There was no way they were leaving the van unattended, not after all the effort they had gone to in acquiring it and stocking it. So they bedded down inside, praying that nobody would wander down the lane and take an interest in them.

They had enough provisions in the van to last them several days. In addition to the cans they had taken from Patricia, they had taken what was left from Hannah's house as well as all the toiletries and utensils they might need.

An investigation of nearby houses the previous evening had led to a couple of confrontations with terrified homeowners convinced Josh and Charlie had come to rob them. Their way around this was to reassure them they were just checking that the neighbours were OK but they were still eyed with suspicion. It didn't help that they didn't live in the street and none of these people had ever seen them before.

A few doors down from Hannah's house they got lucky when trying the door of a house from which they had received no response. It was unlocked, and despite the smell of food that was starting to go off, they found that it was unoccupied. Whoever had lived here had gone, so Lauren and Seema felt no guilt at cleaning the place out.

Their final discussion before departure had been regarding where they were going to go. Before it got dark, the five of them gathered around a good old-fashioned 2003 road atlas which had been sitting neglected on a bookshelf since it had been rendered redundant by satellite technology.

"Just think," said Charlie. "This battered old atlas is more valuable to us now than the most expensive satnav money can buy."

"I always said we should keep physical copies of everything," said Seema. "This whole idea of everything being in the cloud sounds convenient, but what happens when the cloud isn't there anymore?"

"Where are we going to go, then?" asked Lauren, as they pored over the map.

"As we said before, as remote as possible," said Josh.

"Like the Highlands of Scotland?" suggested Kaylee.

"That's way too far," said Josh. "We wouldn't have enough petrol for a start, and the further we go, the more possible problems we could run into."

In the end, they decided that the most remote area within reach was the Cotswolds, and traced out a rough route based on remote country lanes and B-roads. It was Charlie and Kaylee who came up with the suggested choice for their final destination.

"Broadway Tower?" said Josh. "But that's a tourist attraction, isn't it?"

"Yes, Charlie took me there for a day out when we had a romantic weekend away in the country," replied Kaylee.

"I'm sure he did," said Josh, who wasn't into the whole romance thing. "But I'm not sure it's what we are looking for. I was thinking more along the lines of a farmhouse."

"Yes, and won't a lot of other people have that same idea?" said Charlie. "But who would be interested in visiting a tourist attraction right now? Believe me, it's an ideal place. Likely to be deserted and easy to defend."

"What about food?" asked Lauren.

"They've got a café," said Kaylee.

"That's not going to be open, is it?" replied Lauren.

184

"No, but there is farmland all around," said Charlie. "I'm sure we could find food."

"OK, it's as good a destination as any," said Josh. "Now we just need to work out how to get there, staying as far as possible off the beaten track."

With a rough route laid out and the van loaded up, they were ready to depart, bedding down inside it for the first part of the night until they judged it was safe to leave.

At 3.30am, Josh got out of the van and went to check the nearby roads. All seemed quiet so they started the engine and eased cautiously along the lane and through the residential streets that would lead them towards the edge of town.

Charlie and Seema were to share the driving between them and it was she who took the first stint. It was a journey that would have taken barely an hour on the main roads in the past, but they were working on the theory it could take a whole day, bearing in mind the difficulties they were likely to face.

Just getting out of town was problematic. Abandoned cars were everywhere and twice they had to turn around and find another route. And when they saw a man in the headlights running at them with a baseball bat, Seema nearly crashed into a row of parked cars in a desperate attempt to avoid him.

"Bloody hell, be careful," said Josh, who was sitting in the passenger seat. "We don't want to wreck this thing after all the effort we made to get hold of it."

185

"I wouldn't have swerved at all," said Lauren, eagerly leaning forward from behind the two of them. "I'd have carried straight on. Then it would have been down to him. Get out of the way or get run over."

The only other incident before they left the town was when a brick hit the side of the van with a resounding crash that made them all jump. They did not see who threw it or where it had come from, but it was another reminder that the sooner they were out in the country, the better.

It was still dark as they crossed the bypass and onto a minor road that would take them through the village of Chesterton. Seema exercised caution, never going above about twenty miles per hour because the risk of coming across something blocking their path was ever-present. It was also important that they didn't lose their way. Many of the roads they were using were so minor that they didn't have names or signposts.

Frequent stops and diversions meant it took them an hour to reach the village of Upper Heyford, by which time it was beginning to get light. Shortly after leaving the village, heading north, they spotted another vehicle coming towards them.

Josh was taking the role of navigator, and when he spotted the approaching vehicle he knew they were in trouble. It was a black Range Rover which looked disconcertingly like the one he had seen on the day the lorry driver met his demise on the A34.

"This could be trouble," he said with a glance across to Seema. "Whatever you do, keep driving."

The Range Rover was about a hundred yards away when Josh saw the shape of a loudhailer emerge from the passenger side window, followed shortly by an order to pull over.

"Ignore them!" urged Josh, as Seema looked across at him, unsure. "Put your foot down."

When it became clear they weren't going to stop, the Range Rover moved threateningly to block their path.

"I'll have to stop, I'll hit them!" she cried.

"If you stop, we're all dead," insisted Josh.

She kept her nerve and held her line, resisting the urge to close her eyes as it seemed a head-on collision at high speed was imminent. But then, at the last minute, the Range Rover veered off.

"What's happening?" asked Kaylee, who was in the back with Charlie and Lauren, as Seema accelerated away.

"Look out the back window," urged Josh. "Can you see them?"

Kaylee looked out to see the Range Rover reversing into a small turning that led into a field.

"Yes, they're turning around," she said, watching as the vehicle began to follow them.

"Keep driving!" urged Josh to Seema, who had barely recovered her composure following the narrowly averted crash. Even so, she floored the accelerator as she attempted to outrun their pursuers.

"We're not going to get away from them in this," said Charlie as the high-performance Range Rover zoomed towards them. Then the call to pull over was repeated.

"We have to keep going," said Josh. "I think these are the men that killed the truck driver. If they catch us, we may well suffer the same fate."

As if to emphasise his words, the sound of a gunshot rang out. He wasn't sure if it had been fired directly at them or as a warning but it hadn't hit them. But it was enough to send a sense of panic through the group as they realised just how much peril they were in. Seema, behind the wheel, knew the others were relying on her and steeled herself, gripping the wheel harder and figuring that if she couldn't outrun them, she would have to outmanoeuvre them.

"They're almost on us!" shouted a terrified Kaylee, moving away from the rear window, fearful of the possibility of bullets coming through. As she did, Seema skilfully steered the van round a tight turn at speed, desperate to stay in front of them. The Range Rover drew closer, then rammed them from behind, sending a massive jolt through the van, but Seema was unperturbed and kept them on the road, just as they approached a long, straight section.

She put her foot down but the van was no match for the Range Rover which easily drew alongside, and then rammed into them from the side, using their vehicle's sheer muscle to try to force the van into the ditch on the side of the road. She almost lost control at this point as the left wheels strayed onto the grass and it was a battle to maintain control. Then she looked up ahead and realised what she needed to do.

She summoned all her strength for one final roll of the dice. Timing it to perfection, she unexpectedly side-swiped the van back against the left side of the Range Rover, as forcefully as she dared, and it had the desired effect. Windows shattered on both vehicles as the two vehicles collided, but it was the pursuers who came off worse as their car careered off the other side of the road and straight into a massive impact with a large oak tree.

Seema immediately brought the van to a halt, and the five friends jumped out to see what had become of their aggressors. The state of the vehicle suggested it was unlikely they would have any more to fear from them. Despite the strength of the Range Rover, hitting a solid object at that speed had completely crushed the front of it and it was now hissing and steaming due to the burst radiator.

"Careful," said Josh who had seen enough movies to know what might happen next. "It could blow up."

But a cinematic fireball did not ensue, and as they cautiously crept closer they came across a gruesome scene. The bloodied heads of the two men, one of which had almost become detached from the body, told them all they needed to know. Even the airbags, on which their heads now rested amongst a mangled

189

pile of metal, hadn't been able to save them from such a catastrophic impact.

"Wow," said Lauren, seemingly unperturbed by the gore in front of her. "I'm impressed. Where did you learn to drive like that?"

"Milton Keynes," said Seema. "I used to race at a karting track there and won their under-16 championship back in 2012. I wish I'd kept it up really. I had dreams of being the first female F1 champion when I was a kid."

"Well it certainly stood you in good stead today," said Charlie.

"I'm not proud of it," said Seema. "I've just killed two men."

"You didn't kill them. They killed themselves, while they were trying to kill us," said Lauren. "Nobody forced them to chase us and start firing guns at us."

"True enough," replied Seema.

"You did what you had to do," added Lauren. "Just like I did back at my mum's place. Now it's my turn to be impressed."

"Let's take a look around the back," said Charlie.

Although the front of the vehicle had been crushed like a tin can, the rear was relatively unscathed. Now, on opening the boot, they discovered what under the current circumstances could only be described as a treasure trove.

The spacious rear of the car was packed with food, medicines, toiletries, and no end of other things they could make use of. But their eyes were most drawn to the guns, of which there were several.

"Anyone ever fired one of these before?" asked Josh, picking up a pistol. He had never held a firearm before.

They all shook their heads until Lauren piped up.

"No, but I'm more than willing to learn," she said.

"It's time we all learned," he said, handing her the gun before picking out another and handing it to Kaylee, who took hold of it reluctantly.

"Are you sure?" asked Kaylee, curiously running her finger up the barrel and feeling the smooth, cold metal. "Doesn't that make us no better than them?"

"They were using these to rob and kill people," said Josh. "We'll be using them purely for defence. To protect what we have, including all this stuff. It's no use to them anymore."

"Stuff they stole from other people," said Kaylee.

"Who are probably dead, so it's not like we can go and give it back to them, can we?" said Lauren.

"I just don't like the idea of guns and violence," said Kaylee. "Surely there's a better way to do things? I mean, the

191

state of those men. I've never seen a dead body before today and it's simply horrible."

"It's high time you realised this isn't some jolly road trip out into the country," replied Lauren. "There will be plenty of other men like these two out here. You've no room for morals or for getting squeamish. Or you are going to end up as dead as those two."

She felt bad speaking so harshly to her best friend, but sometimes these things needed to be said.

"I suppose so," she replied, before handing the gun to Charlie. She couldn't bear touching the thing.

"Come on, then. Let's get as much of this stuff as we can into the van and get going before anyone else comes along to claim it," said Josh. "If those two were part of a wider group, they are bound to come looking for them."

Doing their best to ignore the two corpses in the front, the team began stripping the wrecked vehicle, eager to get back on their way as soon as possible.

Chapter Thirteen
August 2023

Charlie was the next to disappear.

The team stopped for lunch in a remote spot near the small village of Whichford in Warwickshire. It had taken them several hours to reach this point, and they were all in need of some rest and recuperation after the dramatic car chase. All of them had found the experience harrowing, though some were handling it better than others. Kaylee in particular was still mortified at what she had seen, and Charlie had spent most of the time since consoling her in the back of the van.

The two men might have lost their lives, but their ill-gotten gains hadn't gone to waste. For lunch, the group tucked into some of the supplies they had procured from the Range Rover. What they had taken put their modest collection of tins to shame. Now, they were able to dine on fresh bread, butter, and smoked salmon. There were plenty of other refrigerated goodies too, kept in chiller boxes filled with ice, and even a bottle of champagne, which Charlie promptly opened.

"Do you think we should be drinking champagne bearing in mind the situation?" asked Kaylee, as they all sipped the vintage cru from the multicoloured cheap plastic beakers that came with the campervan. "I mean, it's hardly like we've got anything to celebrate, is it?"

"I think being alive is something to celebrate, don't you?" said Lauren, who was knocking back her bubbly faster than the others.

"But for how much longer?" replied Kaylee. "Even if we do survive this road trip, don't forget the sword that's hanging over all of our heads."

"There is no point dwelling on that," said Josh. "We don't know what's coming, or when. Until then, we've simply got to stay alive. We can't deal with whatever happens after we vanish until we get there."

"If we get there," said Kaylee. She had generally been the most pessimistic throughout the past couple of weeks. Perhaps it had been because of the shocking disappearance of Jess, right back at the start of all this. Even now, after all that had happened since, she still couldn't stop feeling guilty about the disappearance of the girl even though she knew it hadn't been her fault.

Her ominous words almost seemed to pre-empt what was to happen next when Charlie got up to go and answer a call of nature, wandering off into some woods close to where they were parked.

"Where do you think they got this bread from?" asked Seema. "It looks freshly baked to me. And this other stuff has all been kept refrigerated."

"They must have had a base nearby with power," said Josh. "They looked pretty well organised to me."

"You said earlier you thought there might be more of them," said Seema.

"Very probably," said Josh. "Hopefully, we're far away enough now that their friends aren't going to track us down. And even if they do, we've got weapons now, haven't we?"

"And you're prepared to use them?" asked Kaylee.

"If I have to, yes," he replied.

"That goes for me too," said Seema.

"And me," added Lauren.

Kaylee said nothing. She wasn't sure if she was ever going to get used to the stark reality of the new life they were all facing.

"Charlie's taking his time," she said. "I think I might go and look for him."

"Sneaking off for a quickie in the woods, eh?" said Lauren. "I don't blame you. There's not a lot of privacy in this van."

"Hardly," said Kaylee. "That's more your sort of thing."

"True, but I haven't got a willing partner at the moment," she said, looking around at the others. There was Josh, her ex, but nothing had happened with him for a long time. Then there was Seema, who briefly caught her eye and she felt a slight hint of something. She had felt a connection to her before, but was it an attraction? She had had one or two brief dalliances with girls before, but nothing more than messing around. Somehow, she sensed it might be different this time.

Kaylee disappeared into the woods where Charlie had gone, but it wasn't long before she returned.

"He's not there!" she exclaimed when emerging a minute or two later. "I think he's gone to the Rapture!"

"Can we please stop saying that?" asked Lauren. "Nobody has gone to the Rapture any more than they've been beamed up to space. I'm sick to death of hearing about it."

"Who cares what we call it, it doesn't alter the fact that he's gone," said Kaylee, sick at losing yet another person close to her. It couldn't have happened at a worse time, after the traumatic events of earlier.

"We'd better double-check," said Josh. "Seema, can you stay with Kaylee? We can't leave the van unattended. Lauren and I will look."

The two of them headed into the woods, calling Charlie's name, but there was no response.

"Do you think he has gone?" asked Lauren.

"It looks that way."

"Well," she replied, looking at him and sensing an opportunity. "If that's the case, there's nobody around to see or hear us. Kaylee might not have come in here in search of a quickie, but there's no reason we shouldn't."

196

"I thought you said we weren't going to do it anymore," said Josh, who had no intention of turning her down.

"That was before. Let's face it, if this truly is the end of the world, we may as well have a little fun before we go. This could be our last chance."

"Go on then," he said. "For old times' sake."

And they did, briefly, because it had been some time since Josh had last indulged and it was over embarrassingly quickly.

"Well, you did say you wanted a quickie," he said sheepishly by way of apology, as they pulled their trousers back on. They hadn't even bothered taking their tops off.

"Come on," she said, feeling slightly hard done by. "Let's get back to the others."

Strangely, she felt slightly guilty, a rarity for her when it came to sexual matters. She felt almost as if she had been disloyal to Seema, even though there was nothing between them. Part of her was wishing it had been Seema who had come into the woods with her rather than Josh.

The plan had been that Charlie would drive the next stint, but with him gone, Seema had no choice but to resume driving duties. Sticking to the minor roads, as before, they slowly wended their way through the English countryside. By direct route, the journey would have been under forty miles, but as they began the ascent to Broadway Tower, late in the afternoon, Seema noted that they had covered almost a hundred.

They hadn't seen anyone else on the roads for miles, but perhaps given the impassable nature of many of them, it was to be expected. They had been forced to reroute several times, taking them through some settlements they had hoped to avoid, but hadn't seen anyone. This led to some speculation among them as to how many people were left. They did not have access to the projected figures that Jenna and the other ministers had studied.

Kaylee had been inconsolable most of the way. Lauren had tried to be sympathetic but in the end, had snapped at her that she needed to get her act together. After that, she lay down and slept for a while, leaving the others to mull over the events of the day.

Finally, as afternoon turned to evening, they finished the ascent to the tower, pulling into the car park near the café. Normally on a summer day like this, the place would be swarming with tourists but they were pleased to see that today it was deserted.

"Not a day tripper in sight," said Josh, looking at some dark clouds out to the west. "Now we just need to work out how to get inside."

Broadway Tower was an impressive structure situated atop a hill, at one of the highest points of the Cotswolds. They had seen it from many miles away as they had approached, a proud beacon with a commanding view of the surrounding countryside.

Built from local Cotswold stone, it resembled a slender castle with three circular turrets surrounding a central hexagonal section. As the group walked towards it they could see from the windows that it consisted of multiple levels, gradually narrowing towards the top.

"Bagsy the top bunk," said Lauren.

"I'm not sure if there are any bunks or beds of any kind in there," said Josh. "It's primarily a museum these days."

"You're right," said Kaylee, who was beginning to regain some of her composure now they were away from the dangers of the road. "I've been here before, remember?"

"But people used to live in it, right?" asked Lauren.

"Yes, in the nineteenth century, if I remember correctly," said Kaylee.

"Well, we've got the sleeping bags in the van and it's not cold. I'm sure we can make ourselves comfy," said Lauren.

"If we can get in," said Josh.

Remarkably, they could. The arched doorway split into two doors which opened outwards from the centre and when Josh tried one he discovered it had been left unlocked.

"That was a bit careless," said Josh, surprised when he opened the door so easily. "Anyone could just wander in here."

"Like we just did," said Seema.

"Perhaps whoever was looking after this place vanished too," suggested Lauren. "While he or she was here, hence the unlocked door."

"A reasonable assumption," said Josh. "The important thing is, we are in."

"You know, I don't think anyone's been in here for some time," said Seema, looking around the room they had entered. The ground floor served as a gift shop, and all the merchandise was untouched. A lot of what it sold was edible, from local produce to the ubiquitous boxes of fudge that could be found in every tourist shop in Britain.

The stairs were narrow and circular, housed within the turrets, and led up to a first floor which consisted of a large and very posh dining room, with plush carpets and drapes, and windows everywhere through which the sun was still shining.

"At least we can pretend we're eating like royalty," said Josh. "Even if we will be using this posh cutlery to eat tins of beans once all the fresh stuff's run out."

They moved up to the next floor, which was laid out like a living room, as was the next which had some very comfortable-looking furniture. Reading the attached signs, Kaylee noted that these were swanky Hampton Court armchairs from the early twentieth century.

All the furniture was fenced off behind ropes, but Lauren pushed those out of the way and immediately went to sit in one of the chairs.

"Very comfy," she said, before leaping up and heading up to the next floor which turned out to be the roof.

"Damn, no beds," she said. "Still, I could see myself falling asleep in one of those comfy chairs."

The others weren't paying attention, as they were too distracted by the breathtaking views. Plaques around the walls suggested that on a clear day you could see as many as sixteen counties.

"We couldn't have chosen a better place," said Josh. "And we can defend ourselves from up here if we have to."

"Let's hope it doesn't come to that," said Kaylee, still trying not to think about the prospect of having to fight for her life.

"There are definitely worse places we could live out our remaining days," said Lauren.

"Do you really think that's what we're facing?" asked Seema. "This can't be the end of everything, can it?"

"I don't believe it is," said Josh. "I've thought from the start that this is just like what happened with the original time bubble. My theory, for what it's worth, is that the whole world is being sent forwards in time. Why, we won't know until it's our turn."

"I hope you're right," said Lauren, as they gazed out at the landscape stretching out in all directions, still lit up by the

201

descending sun. As they did, she wondered how many more sunsets each of them would see.

She wasn't the only one. All over the world, those that remained wondered how long they had left as the disappearances continued apace. By the time three weeks had passed, barely a quarter of the world's population remained and the lawlessness and the chaos of the last two of those weeks began to subside.

Food shortages were becoming less of an issue with fewer people to feed. Gangs and criminals were also scaling back their activities as they reduced in number, many realising that there was little point to their activities.

Most people concluded that peaceful cooperation was the best way to go. Parents with young children, fearful that they might disappear leaving the child helpless, sought other trustworthy adults in the hope that should the worst happen the child would not be left alone. But every day, these briefly formed communities became smaller.

On the farm, Kent was the last man standing, left alone once Arthur had gone. He diligently looked after the last remaining couple of cows, living off their milk and the odd egg from the rapidly depleting stock of chickens. Then, getting on for a month after it had all started, he too was gone.

The bunker below Downing Street had provided adequate protection to its inhabitants from those outside who had failed in their attempts to break in, but it couldn't stop them from disappearing like everybody else.

To her annoyance, Jenna Rose found that those who were incarcerated with her were in no mood for her totalitarian ways. In the final days, with all the soldiers gone, as well as all the members of her own family, she became vulnerable and was openly scorned by those that remained. She strongly suspected that Dominic was stirring up trouble behind her back, proving himself to be the turncoat she had always suspected him to be.

Those that remained seemed far more interested in the level-headed things that Simon Grant had to say than in her increasingly crazed utterances. When she finally vanished, the five remaining occupants felt a sense of liberation, even though they knew their time was fast approaching.

At Broadway Tower, during a decent spell of hot weather in the second half of August, Seema had taken to sleeping on the roof at night, looking up at the stars. With all power gone, she had never seen the night sky so clearly and found the starry skyscape a thing of beauty to behold. In the week following their arrival, first Kaylee, and then Josh, disappeared. With just her and Lauren left, seemingly alone in the world, inevitably they turned to each other and took to spending their nights together, cuddled up beneath the stars.

Lauren had never been one for romance. She considered it slushy, but she had to admit there was something magical about those nights gazing out into the heavens. Looking out into a cosmos full of an unimaginable number of other worlds made her feel very small, and contrastingly very big at the same time. That didn't really make any sense, but when she tried to explain it to Seema, she knew exactly what she was trying to say.

In the final couple of days, an eerie stillness began to settle upon the world. The growing silence was most noticeable in the complete absence of birdsong, its former continual symphony extinguished. There was also no evidence of any human or animal life in any of the sixteen counties visible from the top of the tower. To the two women gazing out across the landscape, it felt as if it was just the two of them left, custodians of a forgotten Earth where the only sound left was that of the gentle breeze rustling through the trees.

On the first day of September, Seema woke alone, and before sunset that same day she too was gone, one of the final few to depart. The once thriving planet Earth was now completely devoid of animal life.

Then, the following evening, came the extraordinary event that there were no eyes left on the planet to see.

As dusk turned to night, an ethereal luminescence began to emanate from the skies above. A radiant light, vibrant in hues of pink and purple, cascaded around the globe, enveloping every inch of the surface. The world bathed in the eerie glow, almost as if embraced by an otherworldly presence. It flooded every corner of the planet, casting a surreal glow upon the abandoned cities and quiet countryside as it ebbed and flowed in waves, making intricate patterns in the sky.

The pink light even pervaded the depths of the ocean, far beneath where the rays of the sun were able to penetrate. The incredible display persisted for hours before it gradually began to recede. Steadily, it dissipated as dawn arrived at Broadway Tower, leaving behind no remnants of its presence. As the sun rose, the sky returned to its familiar shade of blue, as if it were just another normal day.

Nature, ever resilient, remained unscathed by this celestial spectacle. The plants remained untouched, showing no ill effects from the mysterious light, which had also left the buildings and other vestiges of human civilisation intact.

But of the missing humans, there was no sign.

Chapter Fourteen
September 2023

Jake Rogers didn't deserve the fate that befell him. But then neither did the millions of other people who just happened to be in the wrong place at the wrong time when they were scooped up from their time streams through no choice of their own.

He had been happily cruising down the M40 on a welcome sunny afternoon, looking forward to getting home to a family birthday celebration. Then, he had become the first known person in Britain to disappear.

As far as the world he had left behind was concerned, he had simply vanished without a trace. But for Jake, the experience was quite the opposite.

One minute he was sitting in his cab, enjoying the sunshine pouring in through his open window. The next, he was tumbling towards the tarmac at sixty miles per hour, the protection of the lorry gone. From his perspective, it was not him that had disappeared. It was his truck.

He didn't even have time to react before he hit the ground with a sickening thud, feeling agonising pain shoot through him as countless bones in his body shattered. He rolled over several times before coming to a halt, badly battered, bruised and bleeding. But he was still conscious, just.

Raising his head to look around him, he weakly tried to cry for help, but other than a few abandoned cars, the motorway was deserted. In his debilitated state, he could barely register what was going on, but despite the confusion, he noticed that it was raining and cold, whereas seconds ago it had been bright sunshine.

Feeling the taste of blood rising into his mouth, he knew he was badly injured and needed urgent medical attention but as he felt consciousness start to ebb away, he had a sense of despair that none was coming. He could not see or hear any sign of anyone or anything, and within a few minutes, he was no longer capable of sensing any. He was dead.

For hours, his lifeless body lay undisturbed in the middle of the road, growing colder as the cool rain slowly drenched it. Then, in the sky above, a solitary raven materialised. It sensed the abrupt shift in weather as it mirrored Jake's journey, transitioning from the warm July sunshine into the cool September rain. Momentarily perplexed by the absence of traffic on the usually busy motorway below, it circled, resuming its usual search for roadkill to feast on below.

Spotting Jake's body it cautiously descended, verifying the man's lifelessness before committing itself. Eyes fixated on the blood that had seeped across the road and the gaping wounds that marred the man's flesh, it began pecking at the lifeless body, its hunger overpowering any hesitation. The taste of human flesh, a delicacy it had never encountered before, fuelled its voracious appetite.

It did not need to fly away to dodge approaching vehicles, as was usually the case, since today there were none. The raven was also able to enjoy feasting alone, without having to compete with other scavengers. In this currently empty world, there was not another bird, insect, or creature of any kind in sight.

Over the next few hours, thousands of people across Britain went through the same experience as Jake as they found themselves suddenly thrust forwards in time. Thankfully, not all of them suffered such grisly fates as him, but even so it was very disconcerting for them to find that everyone in the world had disappeared.

In London, on the same afternoon that Jake had disappeared, Lorraine Green had been enjoying her first meeting as the new finance minister for one of Britain's leading high street banks. The boardroom, up on the 84th floor of a stunning new office building in Canary Wharf, had glass windows on three sides, giving stunning views of the busy metropolis below.

During a break in proceedings, she excused herself to visit the loo, and when she returned it was to find the room empty. Of the other board members there was no sign, and there was also no trace that they, or anybody else, had even been there. It was also darker in the room, with black storm clouds threatening outside.

She tried the light switch – nothing. Then she noticed that her laptop was missing, as was her bag which contained her mobile phone. Where was everyone? There was a single landline telephone in the room so she picked that up. It was completely dead. Then she looked out of the window, which was when the realisation that something incredible had happened. It wasn't just the room she was in that had emptied; it was the entire city. There was not a sign of life as far as she could see.

She, and most of the others finding themselves in this strange situation all initially came to the same conclusion. Everyone else in the world had vanished, and there were the only ones left. But as they explored further, they began to find anomalies that suggested that might not be the case.

Back in Oxfordshire, Harry Richards might not have been thrown into an immediate life-threatening situation, but his circumstances were concerning, to say the least. After spending a night in police custody, he had woken up expecting some breakfast at the very least but nobody came to his cell. He tried calling for help, but there was no response. After a few hours, he began to realise that something was very wrong.

"You can't keep me here like this," he yelled through the locked door. "It's inhumane."

There wasn't much in the cell to shed light on the situation, including the light itself which he discovered, just as Lorraine had, did not work. There was still water coming from the tap, but it didn't taste particularly fresh to him and he also noticed when he tried to wash his hands that there was no hot water. Mercifully, the toilet still flushed.

A small amount of daylight was filtering into the gloomy room from a small window, right up close to the ceiling. It was narrow enough that even the slimmest of prisoners wouldn't be able to squeeze through it, even if they had managed to find a way to climb up there.

He had no way of keeping track of time in the cell, and after what felt like a few hours, but was probably less, he concluded that he was going to have to try to break out. That wasn't going to be easy but at least he wasn't in a proper prison. He was confident that if he could get through the cell door it would be plain sailing after that. If there was nobody in the station, as seemed to be the case, getting out ought to be relatively straightforward.

It might only have been one door, but it was a solid metal one. He had no key and no obvious means of breaking it down. He looked around the room for something he could use as a makeshift battering ram but his options were limited. Police cells were not escape rooms. They did not tend to come with built-in tools that clever prisoners could use to liberate themselves.

The only thing that might possibly have any effect was the radiator on the wall, but he had no way of detaching it. He tried tugging at it to see if he could loosen it, but it was a fruitless exercise. Even if he could get it off it was fanciful to imagine it might be able to break down a thick steel security door. Frustrated, he returned to the door and began banging away in frustration, screaming for help as he did. Then, by some miracle, his prayers were answered.

Suddenly, there were the sounds of bolts being drawn back and the cell door being unlocked. It swung open to reveal Sergeant Johnson, the man who had been on duty the previous evening when Harry had been brought in, standing in front of him.

"What the hell is going on?" asked a relieved but angry Harry. "What do you mean by keeping me locked up here for hours on end with no food?"

"Yes, I'm sorry about that, Mr Richards," replied Adrian. "We're a little short-staffed today. Extremely short-staffed, you could say. There is only me, I am afraid."

"In the station?" asked Harry, thoughts of escape running through his mind.

"Not just in the station," said Adrian. "Everywhere. Perhaps you had better come with me and I'll explain. There seems little point leaving you locked up in here under the present circumstances."

Adrian took him into the communal area where the officers usually ate their meals, but there was no food forthcoming.

"Wait a minute, aren't you going to get me anything to eat?"

"I'm afraid there isn't anything," said Adrian. "As you can see, the power's off and there is nothing in the machines."

Harry looked around him, noting a couple of vending machines of the type that normally dispensed sandwiches and other snacks. But the front of it had been smashed open and everything that had been inside had been taken.

"I don't understand," said Harry. "What's going on here?"

"That is a mystery I'm yet to get to the bottom of," said Adrian. "I was called in here this morning because I was told you had gone missing. But when I walked into the station I found that everyone else was missing and it was only you that was still here. The place was deserted, and when I looked outside, everyone there seemed to have vanished as well."

"So what are you saying? That you and I are the only two people left in the entire world?"

"That's a fair assessment of the current position, yes."

"But why?" asked Harry. "Why just us?"

"That, I am afraid I don't know."

"Well, perhaps you should investigate! You're a detective aren't you?"

"A sergeant, as it happens."

"Yes, but you are still a policeman. It's still part of the job description."

"You're right, it is, and what is also part of my job is keeping you in custody. I may have let you out of the cell, but technically you are still under arrest so I am going to have to put you back, while I go and look for some food."

"You must be joking!" said Harry. "What's the point?"

212

"The point is law and order. Whatever is going on outside, I am still responsible for you."

"If there's no one outside, then there is no law and order. There is only you and me. And I'm not going back in that cell."

Catching Adrian off-guard, Harry leapt up and ran for the door that he knew led out to the front of the station. The sergeant thought about giving pursuit but then considered what had been said. What was the point? He would be better off trying to find out what had happened, and rather than worrying about Harry, he was far more concerned about his wife and son. So he decided to go home and check on them.

Adrian and Harry might have thought they were the only two people in town, but others were beginning to show up, scattered far and wide at first. This included Jess, and for her, the experience of finding herself alone and seemingly abandoned at the age of three was bewildering. One minute she had been playing in a sunny garden with her newfound ladybird friends while Kaylee was getting her a drink, the next she saw the ladybirds vanish from her arm and the sun from the sky.

Strangely, she wasn't scared at first, more surprised. At three, she wasn't fully aware yet of what was or wasn't possible in her world and didn't realise the full significance of the sudden change. Her first thought was to go and tell Kaylee, so she jumped up and ran to the kitchen door but when she got there, she noticed something that for the first time sent a small frisson of fear through her.

The kitchen door was hanging off its hinges and was damaged where someone had kicked a hole in it.

"Kaylee?" she called nervously, as she walked slowly into the kitchen. But the room was empty. And not just empty, it was a mess. Drawers had been pulled out and the contents scattered all over the floor, plus the cupboard doors had been left open and stripped bare of their contents. She was still thirsty and needed a drink, but had never made one by herself before. She looked up at the kitchen counter, and the sink towering above her, and noticed her blue cup, teetering on the edge.

She was just able to reach it and knocked it down into her hands. Now she just had to get to the water, but the sink was out of reach. With great difficulty, she managed to drag over a chair and climb up to get to the tap. She had never done this before, but she had seen others do it enough times and three-year-olds weren't babies. They could be remarkably innovative if they needed to.

There was no squash, and the water tasted a little musty, but she gulped it down gratefully. Then she wondered what had happened to Kaylee and the house. Why was it such a mess? Was Kaylee alright? She might have been able to get a drink, but these more challenging questions were outside the range of her understanding. Why had she been left alone?

She wandered around the rest of the house, calling for Kaylee, but with no success. Feeling scared, she retreated to her room and went to sleep for a while, cuddling up to her favourite bear for comfort. She couldn't comprehend what was going on, or why.

214

Later, she got up and went in search of food, but there was nothing in the house. Whoever had emptied the cupboards had taken it all. The fridge was completely empty, and the light did not come on when she opened it. At least she still had water but she was hungry and scared, and in the end retreated once again to her room.

The following morning dawned brighter, but she felt so hungry she realised she couldn't stay in the house without food any longer. She knew the way to the shops, having walked there or been taken in her pushchair many times. She didn't have any money or any way of buying food, but that did not occur to her. She just knew that the shops were where food came from and that there would be grownups there who would help her.

The front door was not locked, so she ventured out into the street. She had never been out of the house on her own before and remembered being told by her mother never to do so, but it did not seem she had much choice. She had thought she might find some people out on the street who might be able to help but it was deserted out there too. Still wearing the clothes she had been in the previous day, she made her way towards the end of the street, but before she reached the end she saw a man emerge from the last house in the row, wearing a backpack.

Unaware of the potential danger she could be placing herself in, she called out to the man.

"Hello," he replied. "What are you doing out here all on your own?"

He seemed friendly enough, so Jess responded.

215

"I've lost my Kaylee, and my mummy's not come home. I'm hungry. Have you got any food?"

"Indeed I have," said the man, taking off his backpack and opening it to reveal a few tins of peaches and corned beef. "It's not a lot, but it will keep us going until we find some more people, won't it?"

"Thank you," said Jess, who even at the tender age of three remembered the manners her mother had instilled in her. "I'm Jess."

"Nice to meet you, Jess," replied the man. "My name's Harry. Harry Richards."

Chapter Fifteen
September 2023

David Choi had become the ninth Prime Minister of Britain in thirteen years, in the spring of 2023. Since a referendum to bring in proportional representation had been approved back in 2011, the old two-party monopoly had been a thing of the past. On the plus side, it meant a lot more people got a voice. The downside was that it was hard to maintain any sort of stable government and this had led to the front door of 10 Downing Street being referred to as the revolving door.

British born, of Chinese descent, David was the country's great hope for a calmer, more stable future, after a series of political scandals and disasters that had plagued his recent predecessors. Winning a leadership contest against the unpopular Jenna Rose a few months ago had cemented his position, and now, for the first time in a long time, it felt as though Britain was moving in the right direction.

Thus, on a sunny weekend in July when for once there was no crisis, no pressing issue, and a feel-good factor pervaded the country, he took himself and his family off for what he hoped would be a relaxing weekend at Chequers.

It had started agreeably as they were joined by friends for a sumptuous dinner, followed up by some rather splendid wines. But in the morning, David woke up to an experience which, although he did not know it, was being played out in thousands of homes across the country.

Just like all the others, he was waking up to an empty world. No people, no birdsong, no electricity, and worst of all, no food.

Mystified by the absence of his wife next to him, bearing in mind he was almost always the earlier riser of the two, he headed downstairs to look for her. It didn't take long for him to realise that something unprecedented was happening.

The dining room, where had wined and dined his friends the previous evening, had been wrecked, with all the furniture smashed. There was graffiti all over the walls and sleeping bags scattered around the room, along with empty food cans. Chequers looked as if it had been invaded overnight by squatters. How or why, he could not explain, but whatever had gone on, as far as he knew he was still the Prime Minister and he had a country of people to lead. Unlike several of his predecessors who were more interested in feathering their own nests than the needs of their citizens, he genuinely felt a sense of responsibility towards them.

That was if he could find them, of course. Looking around the house, he quickly concluded that he was alone. No family, no staff, nothing. It was like the Marie Celeste. So, the obvious next course of action was to try to contact the outside world. His mobile wasn't working and neither were any of the landlines, so he would have to try another way. If there was anybody out there, he would find them.

Just like 10 Downing Street, Chequers was equipped with a secret emergency bunker, and if this wasn't an emergency, he didn't know what was. He had been briefed when first taking office on how to gain access but hadn't expected that he would ever need to.

He made his way into the cellar and to the entrance, where he was pleased to see that the keypad to gain access was lit up, confirming that down here, at least, the emergency power was on. He punched in his code and looked into the camera for the additional facial recognition that was required. Then, the heavy circular access door swung open and he was able to venture inside.

He had been given a guided tour as part of his briefing so knew his way around the bunker. It didn't take more than a couple of minutes to conclude that there was nobody there and had not been for some time. There was no sign that anyone had taken refuge down here. The place was spotless and all the food and other supplies were intact. Whoever had trashed the room upstairs hadn't managed to break in here.

The room David was heading for was the communications centre. If he was going to contact anyone, that was the place to go. In the small circular room, he first checked the computers for internet access, but although the bunker's Wi-Fi system seemed to be functioning normally, there did not seem to be any external access. Then his eyes alighted on the radio transmitter, which looked rather old-fashioned in comparison to the high-tech equipment all around it.

He adjusted the dials, and pressed the transmit button, preparing to speak and desperately hoping there would be someone on the other end. It felt rather odd speaking into dead air like this. Ordinarily, when he gave a speech it was in a room full of people.

"Hello. This is the Prime Minister of the United Kingdom of Great Britain and Northern Ireland. Can anyone out there hear me?"

The speaker crackled with static but there was no response. He waited for a minute or so and then repeated the message. This time, to his relief, a response came through, accompanied by plenty of crackling but clear enough to hear.

"This is Lieutenant Charles Swayne. I can hear you, Prime Minister. Over."

"Lieutenant Swayne, thank God. I need your help. I seem to be the only person left here in the bunker, and I don't know what's happened to the world."

After a brief pause, he remembered to add the word "over."

"I'm afraid it's the same over here, sir. I woke up this morning to find everyone gone. I'm the only one left in the barracks. Over."

"Well, I can't begin to tell you how relieved I am to hear from you, Lieutenant. Can you come over to Chequers immediately so we can get started on figuring this out? How far away are you?"

"I'm at Sandhurst, sir. I'll be with you as soon as I can. Your safety is my number one priority."

"Thank you, Swayne. I will look out for you. Over and out."

Relieved that he was no longer going to be alone, David returned to the living quarters of the bunker and made himself a cup of coffee with UHT milk, which he had with some long-life croissants he found in one of the food cupboards. As he ate, he recalled a time when he had questioned whether it was worth spending large sums of money to maintain places like this. Now, he could see that it had been worth every penny.

It took about an hour for Swayne to arrive, and the first thing that struck David was how young he looked, certainly no older than his early twenties. Despite his youth, the lieutenant knew that right now he held a huge responsibility for the Prime Minister's safety, and took that very seriously.

"I'm sorry for the delay, sir," said Swayne, as David greeted him on the steps of the house. "It took me a while to find a functioning vehicle. Many were missing from the base or out of petrol. I don't know why."

"I'm just glad to see you, Lieutenant. Perhaps together we can get a handle on what is going on here."

"I think we should get back inside the house, Prime Minister," he said. "After all, we have no idea as to the nature of the threat we are facing."

"Quite right," said David. "I'm not sure if you know, but there's a fully equipped bunker with power below here. Perhaps we can figure things out down there. We can also try and make contact with some others. We can't be the only two people left in the entire world."

"Please lead the way, sir," said Swayne, who hadn't known about the bunker. He wasn't at a level where he was privy to that information, but right now that rank was irrelevant. For the moment, at least, it seemed he had become the most senior army officer in Britain.

Down in the bunker they returned to the communications room where Swayne, more tech-savvy than David, made a further attempt to establish an external internet connection. As he did so, something on the computer caught his eye.

"That's odd," he said.

"What's that?" asked David.

"This clock and calendar on the computer. According to this, it's September 5th, 2023. But, when I went to bed last night, it was July 21st.

"Same. Which means?"

"Well, sir, it means that if this clock is accurate, you and I have been transported about a month and a half forward in time."

"But that's not possible, surely?"

"Not by any means we know. But did you notice how much cooler it is outside? I'll be interested to see what time the sun sets tonight. If my theory is correct, it will be much earlier than it was in July."

"The clock could be wrong," said David.

"Do you have any other clocks? Not connected to the system?"

"Yes," said David. "My wife's got a battery-powered LCD clock by the side of the bed. She's had it for years. It tells you the date, time, and temperature. Hopefully, it's still up there, if the squatters didn't trash it. I'll go and check."

The clock was still there and confirmed what the computer below had suggested. Somehow, there were now around forty-five days of their lives that they could no longer account for.

"What are the possibilities then, Lieutenant? First, we've travelled forwards in time. What else?"

"We could have been unconscious for forty-five days," suggested Swayne.

"But how? Or why?" And then he remembered something. The previous afternoon, he had tripped over and grazed his knee. Rolling up his trouser leg to check, he could see that the graze was still there.

"See that?" he said. "I got that playing tennis yesterday. If I had been unconscious for over a month that would have healed up long ago."

"Agreed," said Swayne. "So let's run with the time travel idea for a moment. If we have travelled forwards in time, where is everybody else?"

"Maybe they have done the same?"

"That doesn't explain where they are, though," said Swayne. "Perhaps they are where we left them, back in July. They probably think I've gone AWOL."

"But what about me? I mean, I'm not being grandiose, but I am the Prime Minister. Surely, there would have been a massive search. And this place wouldn't have been abandoned like this. It's like a scene from some post-apocalyptic movie. I'm half expecting a swarm of mindless zombies to come round the corner any moment."

"It is a mystery, sir, but I am sure we can get to the bottom of it. I suggest we get back on the radio. I specialise in communications. Let's try transmitting on a few other frequencies and see if we can get through to anyone else."

It was a frustrating couple of hours reaching out on the radio and only getting static in return but then, late in the evening, Swayne received a response from a brigadier. He was situated at another base, less than forty miles away, and they made plans to meet in the morning.

Brigadier Lang was a veteran officer with over twenty years of experience, and Swayne naturally stood to attention when the senior officer drove up in a Land Rover.

"At ease, Lieutenant. Where's the Prime Minister?"

"Inside, sir, in the bunker."

"Very good, Swayne. Lead the way."

As the three of them enjoyed coffee and more of the long-life croissants, they discussed the strange situation in which they now found themselves.

"So the thing is, Prime Minister, from our perspective, you disappeared yesterday. We conducted a massive search to try and find you but to no avail."

"The thing is, Brigadier, I didn't disappear. Everyone else did," said David.

"Well, that's not how it appeared to us. And you weren't the only one, we were getting reports of missing people all over Britain."

"Presumably, I was another of those," interjected Swayne. "And now, if I correlate all our experiences, I think I've got enough evidence to conclude what is going on here."

"Come on then, lad, let's hear it," said Lang.

"We've already established that forty-five days have elapsed since the time we seemingly disappeared. Sir, you recall the Prime Minister going missing. Then, many hours later, you find everyone else has vanished too."

"Yes, we already know that, Swayne, get to the point."

"Right, so here is what I think happened. The Prime Minister was thrown forty-five days forwards in time. When he

225

got here, it was deserted. That same day, the same thing happened to me. But it didn't happen to you until later, so that's why you knew he had gone. Then, later, you were thrown forward too. I guess that everyone on the base where you were stationed now thinks you are missing too."

"So let's get this clear," said Lang. "We've all been thrown forward in time, but not at the same time. So where are all the other people?"

"I believe that they are going to be transported forward too, sir. It just hasn't happened yet from their perspective. But it has from ours because they've all gone."

"But why?" asked David. "For what purpose? And how? I mean, is it even possible?"

"Not by any science we know," said Swayne. "But we can't deny the evidence of what's happened. For some reason unknown to us, the whole population of Earth is being transported into the future. We've already arrived. Now we just need to wait for everyone else to catch up."

No one spoke for a few seconds as the weight of what he had just said, sank in. David in particular was beginning to come to some very unpleasant conclusions.

"But that could be catastrophic," he said. "I mean, what's going to happen to society? And what's already happened? I mean, look around this place. There have been squatters in here eating out of cans and trashing the place. And there's no electricity. I mean, yes, we've got the bunker and our own power

226

supply. But what about the rest of the world? What are they going to find when they get here?"

"If my theory is correct, then the past few weeks must have been very difficult," said Swayne. "As more and more people were sent forwards in time, there would not have been enough people to maintain the infrastructure. Food supplies would have ground to a halt, there wouldn't have been enough people to keep the trains, hospitals, or anything else running."

"He's right," said the Brigadier. "On the way over here, I drove through Aylesbury. The place is a complete mess. Burnt-out cars, broken windows, rubbish strewn everywhere. It reminded me of when I was stationed out in Iraq, nearly twenty years ago."

If the situation wasn't so serious, David could have made a quip at this point about Aylesbury always looking like that, but he wisely decided not to. This wasn't a joking matter.

"This is serious stuff, isn't it?" he said instead.

"And it's about to get a lot more serious," said Swayne.

"In what way, Lieutenant?" asked Lang.

"I mean, if it was bad for those people left behind before, that will be nothing compared to what they'll face when they arrive here. There's only a few of us at the moment, but what's going to happen when millions turn up in a world where there is no food, no power, and no law and order?"

"Oh my God," said David, contemplating Swayne's words. "It doesn't bear thinking about."

"Well, with all due respect to you both, we need to start thinking about it and fast," said Swayne. "Because if we don't, millions of people are going to die."

Chapter Sixteen
September 2023

While the realisation of the desperate situation the world was in was sinking in at Chequers, back in Oxfordshire, Jess was enjoying some breakfast at the kitchen table back in her home.

She did not properly understand what was going on but the man who had found her in the street had asked her where she had come from, and she had led him back to her house. There, he had produced some tins from his backpack and given her a meal of tinned peaches and Spam. Then, feeling tired, she had gone to bed, while he promised to stay in the house to ensure she was safe until her mother and Kaylee returned.

Jess didn't understand why they had gone away and still felt a little scared, but Harry had assured her everything would be fine. Now it was morning, and it was another canned breakfast, this time tinned pineapple, and corned beef. Harry, sitting opposite her at the table, ate the same but was still unable to tell her where her mother was when asked. All he kept saying was that she would be back soon. Jess wanted to believe him and was glad this man was looking after her, but she wanted her mother.

She would not have long to wait. Just as she was finishing her corned beef, the kitchen door flew open, and there was Hannah in her dressing gown, looking tired and dishevelled but Jess didn't care about any of that.

"Mummy!" she exclaimed, jumping up and running over to her as a look of relief flooded over Hannah's face. They hugged and then Hannah looked up and clocked Harry. As soon as she did, her moment of joy was extinguished, and her expression changed to one of anger.

"You!" she exclaimed, as the same horrific thoughts returned that had gone through her mind after Jess disappeared.

"I never touched her," exclaimed Harry, quick to defend himself, but this only made matters worse.

"Why would you feel the need to say that?" asked Hannah angrily. "I swear if you've touched her…"

"It's OK, Mummy, it's just Harry. He's a nice man. He looked after me until you came back."

"Tell me, baby, did he touch you at all? Anywhere?"

"No, Mummy. He gave me some food, though. I like Spam. Can we get some the next time we go to Tesco?"

"See?" said Harry. "What do you take me for?"

"A sex pest who has a long history of offending against women."

"Women. Not children. You've seen my record. You know that I have never done anything like that."

"So what were you doing with her?"

"She was on her own in the street outside here with nothing to eat. Nearly everyone else on the planet seems to have vanished. I had some food I found in a house not far away, and so I brought her back in here to keep her safe in the hope her family would come back. Which you now have."

"OK," said Hannah, who still felt sick to the stomach that this man had been anywhere near her child, but was beginning to feel reassured that he hadn't done anything to her. "Well, I am back now, and you are still, as far as I know, supposed to be in police custody. How did you get out of the station?"

"Your colleague, Sergeant Johnson, let me go. In a manner of speaking."

"Johnson? He wasn't even there this morning. What is going on? And what do you mean, everyone vanished? It was just a few people."

"Yes, well, I've been thinking about that and I've come up with a theory."

And for the next few minutes, they came to the same conclusion that the Prime Minister and the army officers at Chequers had.

"Right, well thank you for looking after Jess, Harry, but I think you ought to go now," said Hannah, given that their conversation had come to a natural conclusion. "But once things are sorted out, I'll be expecting us to pick up where we left off, back at the station."

"Go? Go where? Look, you haven't been outside yet and seen what it's like. We're not going to be getting back to normal in a couple of weeks, you know. The world as you know it is gone. Think of it like a man whose heart has stopped beating. You can't just restart it and revive him, weeks later."

"What's your suggestion, then?" asked Hannah.

"Other people will be arriving. We need to find them and work together to rebuild things. Otherwise, we're going to find ourselves fighting for our lives in a dystopian hellhole where nobody will be safe."

"What does dystopian mean, Mummy?" asked Jess.

"Nothing good," replied Hannah, horrified at the thought that right now this sexual deviant in front of her was all she and Jess had as an ally in the grim picture he had just painted. She had no choice but to stick with him for the time being.

"We're going to team up then, yes?" asked Harry hopefully.

"For now," said Hannah. "But I'm warning you now if you try any of your old antics again, I'll chop it off. Do I make myself clear?"

"Perfectly," said Harry, who had no intention of getting up to anything under the current circumstances. He knew how precarious the situation was and right now he was prioritising survival above all else.

Finding other people was not going to be easy. All communications were out, and when they did eventually venture outside, it was just to an abandoned world, seemingly devoid of life. Already, weeds were springing up everywhere, beginning the slow process of nature reclaiming the planet.

"Where is everyone, Mummy?" asked Jess, as they walked along the deserted high street.

"Oh, they'll be back," said Hannah reassuringly.

"And that's the problem," said Harry. "What are they going to do when they get here? What are they going to eat?"

"There must be crops in the fields," said Hannah. "September is harvest time, isn't it?"

"Yes, but what's happened to that food without farmers to look after it? It could be rotting away by now. It's going to take a lot more than getting a few people out to the farms to sort all this lot out."

"Someone in authority must know something, surely?" she replied. "Or be prepared for this? I mean, someone made all this happen, didn't they?"

"I don't know," said Harry. "I think probably not, because surely they would have given us some warning or helped us prepare."

"I can't believe all of this has happened by chance," said Hannah, as the three of them walked on towards the police station.

"Perhaps they didn't know, Mummy," said Jess, who was clutching her mother's hand tightly, not wanting to lose her again.

Jess was right, they didn't. But plans were now being put in place. Between them, the Brigadier and Prime Minister were debating what needed to be done, and it was not going to be pretty.

"Are we sure we want to do this?" said David Choi. "I mean, as a free country, it's hardly what we stand for, is it?"

"Believe me, there is no other way," replied Lang. "Yes, it's going to be tough, and yes, it's going to be cruel, but the survival of the human race is at stake."

"I get that, but what you are talking about equates to modern slavery."

"It's not forever, sir. Just until things are under control."

"Said every power-mad dictator in history," replied David.

"It's just the way my military mind works," said Lang. "I was trained this way."

"So how exactly are we going to enforce this plan of yours with only three people?" asked David.

"Oh, we won't be only three for long," said Lang. "Swayne is down in the bunker right now getting in touch with bases all over the country. We've got soldiers popping up left, right and centre, and what's more, we've got emergency power."

"And how long is that going to last?"

"Long enough for us to get organised, I hope. Like I was saying before we have three priorities. First, get the power grid back up and running. Second, re-establish a reliable communications network. And third, make sure we have enough food to feed the population."

"Food only comes third?"

"How are you going to distribute it without the first two?"

"Fair point, I suppose. And you say we've got a lot of food in storage?"

"Yes, it's one area where foresight is going to come in very handy. Some of our military bases are packed to the rafters with emergency rations. We've been stockpiling and maintaining them for years. The idea behind it was that if some calamity ever befell Britain, we would have enough food to feed the population via any means we could get it to them. For example, if the country got blanketed in metres of snow, we could drop parcels from the sky.

"How much food?"

"Well, enough to get us through the initial hump, though the more people come back the greater the demand is going to be."

"And we can prioritise growing more? I mean, humans lived off the fat of the land for centuries before the Industrial Revolution."

"True, but the population was a lot less then, and there was a lot more agriculture. Most of our food now is imported and packaged. We don't go out into the fields, get our own wheat, and mill our own flour anymore, do we?"

"More's the pity," said David. "Ironic, isn't it? If this had happened three hundred years ago we'd be a lot better equipped to deal with it than we are now. I always thought the more reliant we became on technology, the more vulnerable we were. I think I've just been proven right."

"I'm sure there are lessons to be learned, sir. But right now, we've got a country to rebuild. And if we don't do it, someone else will," he added ominously.

"How do you mean?" asked David. "As in criminal gangs?"

"Not just that," said Lang. "I'm talking about national security. Think about those countries that are more authoritarian than us. What do you think would happen if some of them got themselves organised more quickly than we did? They'll be short of food too. Who is to say they won't see us in the West as weak and easy pickings? We could be facing an invasion within months."

"I hadn't thought of that," said David. "The world has just become an altogether more dangerous place."

"Without a doubt, sir. Do you remember that doomsday clock they used to use to demonstrate how close humanity was to extinction? Well, we are barely a second away from midnight now. What happens over the next few weeks is critical."

"The thing I can't get my head around is just how many people are going to die," said David. "I know you said that you military types are trained to be realistic about these things, but I'm the leader of the country. I have a duty to these people."

"Do you think I don't know that?" said Lang. "I'd dearly love to save each and every soul on the planet but we have to accept we're in an impossible situation. All we can do is save as many as we can."

"Can you give me a realistic estimate?"

"This is an unprecedented event. Any numbers I come up with will be pure guesswork."

"Guess, then. At least give me something to work with."

"OK. Let's say we do nothing and let nature take its course. I believe it will be horrible. Savage, barbaric and brutal. Put it this way. We could well revert to the Dark Ages. Do you know how many people were in Britain at the time of the Norman Conquest? About two million. I could see us going back to something like that."

"Out of seventy million? That's not far off extinction."

"And that's not even taking into account the rest of the world."

"And if we enact the plan, as you've laid it out?"

"Then a lot of people are still going to die. But we could at least save most of the population. Maybe as many as 80 or 90%. I mean, we must try, mustn't we? If we've any hope of ever restoring anything remotely akin to the old infrastructure we are going to need those people to run things.

"How many?" asked David. "What's the minimum we would need?"

"Again, it's only guesswork but 50% is a good ballpark figure. But even if we do manage to get things up and running again, we're in for some very hard times. Forget the Great Depression, or post-war rationing, this is on a whole other scale. It will likely be years if not decades before we return to anything resembling normality."

David considered what had been said, weighing up his options. It seemed he had little choice but to do as the Brigadier had suggested.

"Very well then, Lang. Let's make a start."

Chapter Seventeen
September 2023

Lang hadn't been exaggerating with his statement that a lot of people were going to die. As the population began to return, those unlucky enough to be in the wrong place at the wrong time paid for it with their lives through no fault of their own.

Many who had been travelling suffered a similar fate to Jake Rogers. Falling out of a lorry might have been bad, but for those who suddenly found themselves in mid-air at 30,000 feet, death was quick and cruel. They died terrified and mystified, with no concept of what had happened to them, most of them long before they hit the ground.

For others, dependent on care, it was a slow and traumatic demise. Patients in hospital, denied the essential life support they needed, quickly expired. The old and infirm in care homes, many with dementia, suffered a confused and lonely death. And most tragic of all were the babies, snatched from their mothers' arms and left abandoned, crying for the milk that would never come.

But for every tragedy, there was a heart-warming tale of rescue and human kindness. Some babies had their cries for help answered, as adults returning to the world overheard, rescued and cared for them until they could be reunited with their families.

Gradually, the growing number of returnees began to find each other and form small groups to try to help each other, but the odds were stacked against them. Food was scarce, though there were at least seasonal fruits around for those knowledgeable enough to find them. Unfortunately, just as during the period when people were disappearing, some were more ruthless in their approach, and small gangs once again began to form.

On the second day following her return, Hannah had found Adrian, and along with Harry, whom she had given the benefit of the doubt for the time being, the three of them had decided to form a proper community. While they were out exploring the town to see what resources remained, they discovered a hotel on the edge of town that was one of the few places that hadn't been trashed. From there, they began scouring the streets for new arrivals, who by now were popping up all over the place.

In addition, they put up handwritten posters all over town directing anyone who read them to where they could be found. By the third day, their group had grown to over twenty people, who were grateful for the safe haven that the hotel provided, and for the food, which remarkably had remained untouched, unlike almost everywhere else in the town. It was mostly cereals and large catering packs of canned goods such as baked beans, but it was enough to feed them for a few days while they worked out what to do next. Then, on the fourth day, everything changed.

It was less than a week since the first people had returned, but already there were enough army personnel back to put together a skeleton force. To move around they needed fuel and had learned how to extract it manually from beneath abandoned petrol stations, thanks to a petroleum engineer who had offered his services early on.

He had been recruited on the second day from a village close to Chequers at first, but with his help, and military communications now restored across the UK, they were now ready to roll out their plans on a national basis.

It was late on an unseasonably warm afternoon when a convoy of military vehicles rolled into Hannah's town. Using loudhailers, they called on the residents to come out into the streets, with the promise of food and protection. Some were suspicious and hid away, feeling they were unable to trust anyone after all that had happened. But most, including those who had been staying at the hotel, saw this as a moment of salvation. They knew the food they had could not last forever, and now the army had arrived, everything would be alright. Perhaps overoptimistically, many believed they would now get an explanation for what had happened, and everything would go back to normal.

It was Lieutenant Swayne who was leading the convoy, a level of responsibility somewhat above his station, but with the forces spread so thin, many junior officers had been required to step up to the plate.

After circling the town and calling everyone into the market square, that was where the convoy eventually stopped and Swayne stepped out of the vehicle, fully aware of the huge weight of responsibility that had been placed upon him. Hoping that he would be able to command the authority he needed, at the fresh-faced age of twenty-one, he climbed on top of his jeep where he could be seen by all.

There were hundreds of the townsfolk in attendance, emphasising just how quickly the population was returning. Among them were Hannah and Adrian who were both in police uniform, something they had elected to do as part of their own plans to restore law and order. Alongside Hannah was her daughter who was clutching her mother's hand. They had barely been parted for a second since being reunited.

Swayne raised his hand, beckoning the people to come closer so that they could all hear him before he began speaking "My name is Lieutenant Swayne, and I am in charge of the task force for this area. We are here to offer you food, shelter, and a chance to rebuild our world," he announced, seemingly with good intentions, but Hannah's eyes were drawn to something that made her feel unwary. Swayne was holding a machine gun. Why did he need that in front of his own citizens?

She exchanged a wary glance with Adrian, clutching Jess protectively, but he seemed happy enough, as did most of the rest of the crowd. Then a woman she recognised spoke out. "Why should we trust you?" she asked, her voice laced with hard-edged scepticism.

What she said didn't surprise Hannah in the slightest. The spiky-green-haired woman was well known to her. Her name was Jodie and she was a local political activist mostly relating to climate change issues and had been involved with many protests in recent years. She had been arrested on at least three occasions, once by Hannah herself. Like Lauren's mother, Patricia, she had a deep distrust of authority, but hers came from the opposite side of the political spectrum.

Swayne nodded understandingly, keeping his gaze steady. "I can't promise it'll be easy. But we have a chance to mend what's broken, restore power and grow food. We need engineers, farmers, and skilled individuals who can play their part in this rebirth. Together, we can overcome the mammoth task that faces us all, but divided, we face extinction."

His words hung in the air, and slowly, the crowd started to absorb their meaning. Then, a man with scruffy blond hair stepped forward, eagerly, and spoke. "I studied engineering at university and worked in the energy industry for many years. Getting the power back on is a massive undertaking but I know what needs to be done. With enough of the right people, we can do it," he offered with determination.

"What, so we can all go back to polluting and destroying our world?" said Jodie. "Don't you realise, the one thing people like me have been campaigning for all these years has finally happened? We've stopped oil, and we've stopped burning fossil fuels. This is exactly what needed to happen to save humanity. The old world was corrupt, greedy and on a path to self-destruction. Now we can build a cleaner, greener world!"

Several in the crowd looked towards Jodie and murmured their agreement, which was not what Swayne wanted to hear.

"I admire your idealism," he said. "But the harsh reality is this. The old world may not have been perfect but it kept you all alive, and living comfortable lives. What this lady here is telling you may sound like a utopian, back-to-Eden type of future, but the harsh reality is that it will lead to poverty and death for the vast majority of you. Now she may believe that is a price worth paying for a fresh start, but I don't."

"Me neither," said the engineer. "If you want my help, I'm in."

"Well, I'm not," said Jodie. "I'm not doing anything to help rebuild your patriarchal, big-dick, gas-guzzling world. I'm going to live off the land."

"I'm sorry, but you don't have any choice," said Swayne.

"Why, what are you going to do, shoot me?" she asked. "I wondered why you had the artillery on show. Is this the reason? Do what the man says, or it's up against the wall?"

Swayne sighed. He had hoped it would not come to this but it did not look as if the woman was going to back down, and he was under orders. He was going to have to spell it out.

"Look, the facts are these. As of three days ago, the country is under martial law, by decree of the Prime Minister. Every citizen is obliged to do their bit. Think of it as like helping the war effort. All of you here are going to be assigned to whatever job best suits your skills until such time as we have restored a functioning society."

"And if I refuse, you'll shoot me, right?"

"No," said Swayne. "I will not. But I should point out that under the emergency regulations, all possessions and property are now the assets of His Majesty's Government. If you try to live outside the system then you need to be aware of the consequences. For example, simply by picking fruit from a tree, you will be considered guilty of stealing from the state, which is now a capital offence. And then you will be shot. So I suggest you think very carefully before making your choice."

The mood of the crowd had considerably cooled, at the realisation that for the foreseeable future things were not going back to normal, and that there was effectively no longer any such thing as freedom.

"And how long will this go on for?" asked Jodie.

"Until we get back to normal," said Swayne.

"And who will decide when that is? When we're still all slaves ten or twenty years from now, because it suits whoever is in charge to keep it that way, who is going to be in any position to challenge the status quo? I don't need to quote you examples from history, it's littered with them."

"Those are not my decisions to make. I am concerned only with the here and now."

"Just following orders, eh?" she said, turning to the crowd. "You're not all going to go along with this, are you?"

"What choice do we have?" said the engineer. "You may have hated the old world, but I didn't. I want a warm bed and food and hope for the future. Not starving to death in the wild,

245

risking being machine-gunned if I so much as take a blackberry off a bush."

"There's a question I would like to ask," said Adrian, still standing next to Hannah, taking in everything that was being said. "I want to help with the war effort, so to speak, but if we are all to be deployed where we are best needed, what are the implications for our families? I've got a wife and a son who have not turned up yet. What if you decide you need to deploy me elsewhere and I'm not here when they return?"

"We will document everything and everyone," promised Swayne. "No one need be separated from anyone longer than is absolutely necessary."

"And who decides the definition of necessary?" asked Jodie.

"That is a matter for the regional officers who will be put in charge of each area," said Swayne, neatly absolving himself of any responsibility.

Hannah had been listening carefully to all of this. She did not like the idea of surrendering her freedom to the army any more than Jodie did, but she recognised that it was the only way forward. It wasn't just about her survival, she had Jess to think about too. What kind of life was she going to have if society could not be salvaged? Short, miserable, and brutal. Despite her career in the police force, she had never been a fan of authoritarianism. But in this case, there was no choice. It was time to step forward and speak up.

"People, I recognise that there are concerns with what Lieutenant Swayne is proposing. But unless we work together, we face a very bleak future. Probably, no future at all. I know giving up our freedom temporarily is not something any of us want to do, but I promise you, as soon as things are up and running again, I will be first in the queue to ensure we take that freedom back. So I'm in."

"Of course you are," said Jodie condescendingly.

"Jodie, I know how strongly you feel on many issues, but please, now is not the time to have that battle. Right now, you need to live to fight another day. Do you understand?"

Hannah hoped she would. Despite Jodie being a thorn in her side in the past, she admired the woman's spirit.

Jodie said nothing, but just nodded almost imperceptibly, as others murmured their agreement, much to Swayne's relief. When he joined the army, he knew that one day he might have to turn a gun on an enemy. No one would become a soldier if they weren't prepared for that eventuality.

But he had never envisaged a scenario where he might be forced to fire upon his own people.

Chapter Eighteen
September 2023

Across the country, meetings similar to the one in Hannah's town were taking place, and the returning people were being assigned to their new roles.

A few key people, such as the engineer who had spoken up during Swayne's request for skilled people, were categorised as priority workers, given a higher status, and relocated to where they were needed. But for the majority, the only practical course of action was to deploy their skills locally. Petrol was a precious commodity and not a drop could be wasted moving people around unnecessarily. It also made sense when it came to accommodation. Most people were able to go back to living in their own homes. Even though they had no heating, no hot water, and few of the other creature comforts they had before, at least they were in familiar surroundings with a roof over their heads and a bed to sleep in.

In Hannah's town, various hubs were set up in church halls, sports halls, and schools, where every citizen was expected to register, given an extensive interview, and then assigned to whatever task their skill sets suggested they were suited to. This meant manual labour for many, with the most common task being working on farms to salvage what remained of the season's harvest.

Some in key essential roles, such as doctors and nurses, resumed similar roles to before. But others found that there was no need for their jobs in the new world. Beauticians, solicitors, and advertising executives were just three examples of professions that were considered superfluous in the new world.

Those valued most highly now were the engineers, the farmers, and the electricians. In short, those people who knew how things worked.

One of the most contentious issues, in a largely compliant population, was what to do with the children. It was a controversial decision, but it was decreed that all schooling would be suspended for the immediate future and that all children over ten should contribute to the restoration effort. This would also free up their former teachers to toil in the fields and elsewhere where manual labour was needed. Those under ten would be cared for by those too old for work. Many complaints were voiced about this, with the harsh new reality being compared to sending children up chimneys in Victorian times. But in the end, the people just had to get on with it.

Every citizen was issued with a ration book, and the rations were scarce. Punishments for stealing food were also draconian. If someone in the fields was caught helping themselves to produce, they would not eat for the rest of that day. In a population so used to freedom, the new regime was a shock, but remarkably, most of the people knuckled down and did what they were told.

The days were long, and the work was hard. Most people worked at least twelve hours a day and were too exhausted to do much else. Leisure time was practically non-existent, not that there would be much to do with it anyway. Distractions like television, social media, and pretty much every other form of entertainment no longer existed.

Those in charge knew that they had to show positive progress quickly if the people were to remain compliant, and the top priority was to get the power back on. As communications with other countries began to become re-established, it quickly became clear that sourcing gas and oil, with the whole world desperate for it, was going to be difficult. The focus switched to self-sufficiency, in particular renewables, but these were not enough to power the whole of the UK alone, especially if the wind didn't blow and the sun didn't shine.

The engineers heading up the project to restore the power grid warned what a mammoth project it would be, and how supply would be haphazard and intermittent, possibly for decades to come. But David and his growing group of ministers at Chequers knew that would be better than nothing. Even a partial restoration would go a long way towards reassuring the people that normality was returning.

Eventually, after a monumental undertaking, electricity supplies were restored to large swathes of the country, around three weeks after Lieutenant Swayne and his colleagues had begun the recruitment process. It was just as well because autumn was well underway and the weather was growing colder by the day.

The supply was extremely unreliable at first. The power was only on for a few hours a day at best in most places, but this sent out a clear signal that things were getting better and gave the people the boost they needed to keep going.

Things might have been improving, but life was still brutal and hard. Death was a daily occurrence, from the horrors of dead bodies falling out of the sky, or out of other moving vehicles, to those who couldn't care for themselves and hadn't been found in time.

There were many other problems to deal with too. The returning birds, animals and insects were returning to situations that they were not suited to. Their lives were governed by the calendar and many had missed their migrations, failed to mate at the right time, or found that their food supply had dried up. But nature would in time correct these things, just as it did after a record-breaking cold winter or a drought.

By the beginning of October, the people returning were arriving in a world with more people in it than the one they had left. Unlike the first returnees, there were plenty of people around to tell them what had happened, and they were quickly directed to the local centres to be assigned. For many, this was a distressing process, as they had no idea where their families were. To be told to go off and work on a farm, when they had no idea if their husband or wife was still alive was upsetting, but all the powers that be could promise was they would do their utmost to reunite people as soon as they could. It was largely words, though. The work they needed to do was considered more important than any emotional attachments.

Every individual's experience was different, depending on the circumstances when they left, and when they arrived. In the case of Debbie Kent, who had disappeared early on, she was initially unaware of what had happened. On the morning of her

251

return, she made her way downstairs to the pub to discover the place completely trashed. Every bottle in the place had been drunk or smashed, the furniture was all broken, the windows had been put through, and somebody had taken a dump on top of the pool table.

It was heartbreaking, and when she went outside she was immediately picked up by an army patrol who explained the situation and took her to a nearby school for registration. When she told them she was a cook who ran a restaurant for a living, she was assigned to a local soup kitchen to dole out meagre rations to the hungry population. Her pleas to the army to find her husband fell on deaf ears. They had no idea where he was, all they could tell her was that he wasn't registered. She was allowed to go back to the pub to sleep, but there was no question of it opening again as a commercial premises any time soon.

As police officers, Hannah and Adrian were obvious choices for leadership roles in the local community and were assigned as such, though Hannah baulked at some of the things she was asked to do. The army insisted that she adopt a zero-tolerance approach and exact swift punishments on transgressors of the rules. She reluctantly agreed, as did Adrian, but she was only paying lip service to it. So when she saw a frail, elderly lady who had been sent to pick apples sink her teeth into one of them, she looked the other way.

The thing Hannah hated about the strict regime was how little time she got to spend with Jess. They had been permitted to return to their old house, but she had to get up at half past six every morning, drop Jess off at the day centre where hundreds of children were cared for by a handful of pensioners, and then pick her up at half past eight in the evening. She worked fourteen hours a day, seven days a week, and there was precious little time to do anything else, except sleep.

Was it better to have been one of the first taken, she wondered? What had it been like for Josh and the others who had not yet returned? It must have been tough for them, in a world where the number of people was dwindling and society was breaking down. But then, this was tough too. She was working almost every waking hour and it was wearing her down. She didn't know how much longer she could keep it up.

Every person, when they did return, went through a similar thought process. In most cases, apart from those unfortunate enough to meet with violent accidents, there was relief they there were not dead, had not ascended to the Rapture and had not been abducted by aliens. This relief tended to be short-lived once they realised what sort of world they had come back to.

As soon as he could, David returned to Downing Street. When he saw the dilapidated state London was in, he didn't feel at all confident that the world was ever going to go back to the way it was before. The entire country was living on the breadline, and despite the progress of getting the electricity back on, the challenges of sourcing enough fuel and food for the years ahead were daunting. He knew that maintaining authority was going to be a huge challenge, and not just over the general population either. By now, some of those who had been holed up with Jenna in the bunker had returned. When he heard how

Jenna had behaved, it made him realise just how precarious his situation was. What was going to happen when she returned? The last thing he needed was to have a power struggle on his hands.

Fifty or so miles away from Westminster, on Arthur's farm where Andy and Kent had taken shelter, Andy was the first to reappear. He had gone to bed the previous evening drunk, and feeling sexually frustrated after being holed up for so many days without so much a glimpse of a woman. He was still clinging to his deluded fantasy that the world must be full of lonely women desperate to sleep with him and had decided he was going to go into town later to see if he could find one.

When he woke up, he didn't initially realise what had happened because the room he slept in was largely unchanged. It was only when he got downstairs he noticed that things weren't as they should be.

It was cold, and he could see from the raindrops on the window that the weather had changed. The wood burner in the kitchen had gone out and there was no sign of Kent or Arthur. When he ventured out into the yard, he was greeted with the sight of an army jeep rolling into the muddy farmyard. The vehicle came to a halt, and from within emerged a female officer, her uniform crisp and immaculate, with hair tied up neatly in a bun.

With her were three civilians, two women and one man. In contrast to the officer's sharp appearance, they looked weary and had an unkempt appearance, with grubby clothes and hair that looked as though it had not been washed for several days.

Not that Andy had anything to criticise on that front. He looked like that most of the time and had done even when hot baths and washing machines were freely available.

"Are you the proprietor of this farm, sir?" asked the young officer, as she disembarked from the vehicle.

"Indeed I am," said Andy, seizing on the opportunity to take advantage of Arthur's absence, while looking the young woman up and down appreciatively. "And if I may be so bold, can I just say, you look gorgeous in that uniform."

Andy usually just about got away with these remarks in the drunken banter environment of the pub but it wasn't going to cut any ice here.

"No, you may not," she said. "What do you do here?"

"Milk cows, mostly," said Andy, looking over to the cowshed, which seemed devoid of life. "Though, I am not sure where they are at the moment."

"Running around loose in the lane, it seems," she replied. "We nearly ran into one of them on the way here. Is it just you here?"

"Yes, I have two farmhands, but they seem to have disappeared," he replied.

"It's probably the other way around," replied the officer. "Do you know what's happened?"

"Yes, people are vanishing," said Andy.

"And now they're reappearing," she said. "It's a long story, these three can fill you in after I've gone. Meet your new farmhands."

"Eh?"

"I'm requisitioning this farm under emergency powers granted to me by the British Government. You can stay here and supervise operations, with these three to help you. Can you accommodate them?"

"Yes, well there's plenty of room in the farmhouse."

"Good. Get those cows rounded up and get milking. Plus, we're going to need everything else you produce. I will bring more workers tomorrow, and we'll set up a proper production and collection routine."

"Now hang on a minute, love…" he began.

"Don't argue with her," said one of the women on the truck, a downtrodden, middle-aged lady who looked as if she hadn't washed for days.

"That's right. Don't argue with me, and don't call me love. You work for the government now. We need every single scrap of food and drink this farm can supply and we need it immediately. Do not be tempted to eat any of it yourself. We will allocate you rations."

"But that's outrageous!" protested Andy. "You can't do that!"

"She can," said the woman on the truck. "They've already done it to the rest of us. I haven't seen my brother for weeks. I don't even know if he's alive."

"That's enough, Maria," said the officer. "You all know what the score is. You do as you are instructed or you face the consequences."

The officer stayed long enough to register Andy and take notes on what the farm produced, and then left him in charge, with instructions on what she expected to find when she returned the next day. Only when she was gone, did the others find the courage to speak again.

All three had sorry tales to tell of how life had gone since they had emerged at the other end of their trips through time. As the four of them worked to get the cows back into the milking shed, Andy was filled in on the full story of what had happened.

"But what they are doing sounds like slavery," he said.

"It's not far off it," said Maria. "But what else can we do when the only alternative is death?"

All four of them reluctantly agreed that they had no choice but to comply, but, as they reflected, it could be a lot worse. Andy certainly had no intention of being all authoritative and they were sure there must be many other people in far worse places than they were.

They made good progress throughout the day and managed to milk the cows now they were back in the shed. The weather was much cooler than it had been during Andy's first stint on the farm, which meant the milk would keep longer. With the power coming on for a couple of hours in the afternoon, Andy was hopeful they might be able to get the cold storage facilities up and running again, but the supply was very intermittent.

While Andy was teaching Maria how to milk a cow, he took a glass, dunked it into the bucket and downed it. When she saw this, she initially rebuked him.

"What are you doing? You can't drink that. What if they catch you?"

"How are they going to catch me? Here, have some. It's much nicer than the stuff you get in Tesco."

"But if you're caught they punish you. If you steal food, you're stealing from all of us."

"That sounds like propaganda to me. Did they drum that line into you?"

"They say it all the time. I heard that one man who was caught with a tin of tuna was put in a cage and starved for three days."

"Do you really believe that? It's just a scare story, to frighten you, if you ask me."

"I don't know what I believe anymore. All I know is that I am so hungry."

"Then have some milk. It's full fat, straight from the cow. I won't tell if you won't."

He dipped the glass back into the recently filled bucket and handed it to her. She needed no second invitation, and lifted the vessel to her lips, catching the aroma of the milk. It had seemed such a mundane thing in the past, like bread or butter, but now it was the most gorgeous, desirable liquid in the whole world.

As she drank, the warm liquid flowed over her taste buds, better than any milk she had ever tasted before. This was not the cold semi-skimmed pasteurised stuff she had been buying in plastic bottles for so many years. This was creamy, full, and fresh from the cow. She drank greedily, savouring every drop, and when the glass was empty, Andy refilled it for her. She looked at him gratefully, appreciating his act of kindness. Despite his scruffy appearance and his sexist remarks to the officer earlier, she couldn't help feeling an affinity with him.

"If you enjoyed that, I've got something even better for later," said Andy. "Something that army officer doesn't know about and isn't going to know about if I have my way."

He was as good as his word and much later that evening, when all the work was done and night had fallen, Andy unveiled the farm's plentiful supplies of cider. For the first time since their return, his three new recruits were able to relax and let off some steam.

When the officer returned with more workers the following morning, the remaining cider was safely hidden away and Andy pretended to be fully cooperative with all the instructions given to him. Then, once the authorities were out of the way, he did his own thing. They had no way of monitoring what went on there. Unlike big cities, there wasn't any CCTV to spy on people here. And they knew nothing about farming either. Neither had Andy, until recently, but he knew a damn sight more than them.

He had worked out the best way to play this game and the people who came to the farm appreciated it. He did not crack the whip the way the army had told him to because he did not need to. Everyone worked hard and there was the reward of fresh milk, cider, and other produce from the farm which they wouldn't get anywhere else.

In the meantime, he and Maria grew closer. It had been years since Andy had enjoyed any sort of romantic liaison with anyone, but now, away from the pub and with a renewed sense of purpose, he was beginning to become a significantly more likeable person than before. When the two kissed, a few nights after her arrival, he could scarcely believe it. It was something he had feared would never happen again.

When Arthur returned, he was initially grumpy that Andy had usurped him as top dog on the farm but when he explained the situation, he could see that Andy had gone about things the best way. With his expertise, they were able to improve the yields they were getting from the fields as well as planning for the following year, the importance of which Arthur could not stress highly enough.

Finally Kent returned, by which time over twenty people were working on the farm, more than Arthur had ever employed. By now, the army had assisted in converting one of the barns into a dormitory. Petrol was still in desperately short supply and it made sense to have people living at or within walking distance of their workplaces wherever possible.

When Kent registered, he inquired about the whereabouts of his wife, but the information from the army was not forthcoming. They just said they would look into it, but every time he asked about it he was fobbed off. It was obvious that weren't interested. Eventually a new arrival at the farm, an occasional drinker in the pub in the old days, informed him that she was working as a cook in the town. When Kent asked if he could see her, the request was refused.

He wasn't massively bothered about this, because at least he knew she was safe. They were not exactly love's young dream and if she had been at the farm, she would probably just have nagged him or told him off for drinking too much cider. If they must live apart because of the emergency, who was he to question the wisdom of the powers that be? That would be the excuse he would use when she did eventually catch up with him, anyway.

For others, being separated from their loved ones was a real issue and it caused a lot of pushback against the authorities, who had been ordered to prioritise the recovery effort over all else. Their view was that personal considerations had to be put on hold. This created feelings of resentment among many. A few

261

officers recognised this, and through small acts of kindness, made the effort to redeploy people in the hope of reuniting them.

But others were not so kind. There were some now in positions of power who relished the authority they had over other people and took pleasure in seeing others suffer.

And none craved that power as much as Jenna Rose.

Chapter Nineteen
October 2023

One by one, the five travellers who had set off for Broadway Tower back in the summer began to return.

The first to reappear was Charlie, who had nipped into the woods to answer a call of nature partway through the journey. He knew instantly that he had been taken, by the change in the environment around him. The woodland setting was the perfect setting to demonstrate this, most notably with the tree right in front of him. When he had stopped to unzip his flies, the leaves on the tree had been a rich shade of green, full of vitality.

Now, in full flow, he witnessed an instantaneous metamorphosis into a rich tapestry of warm colours. Although many of the leaves were still green, plenty more had changed to shades of yellow and orange, a sure sign of the onset of early autumn.

Looking up, he could see that clusters of conkers had appeared, concealed within their spiky green husks. Charlie always thought they looked rather like testicles, dangling from the tree's branches ready to unleash their seed. Puerile comparisons aside, the important point was that they should not be this large in August. Charlie's best guess from looking at the tree was that he had arrived in late September or early October. Josh had been right all along. The missing people were travelling forward in time.

He had worked this out more quick than most people but then he had previous experience of this sort of thing. He rightly surmised that the camper van was probably long gone, which was confirmed when he emerged back onto the road and it was nowhere to be seen. What should he do now? Continue towards Broadway Tower? If the others had been sent to the future too, they probably wouldn't be there, but maybe the van would. Chances are this was all irrelevant now, but he might as well trudge on.

Feeling slightly wary, not knowing what the state of the current world might be, he began to tentatively walk along the road, hoping to find some signs of civilisation.

He did not have to wait for long. After he had been walking about half an hour he approached a small village, and that was where one of the regular army patrols, charged with picking up the daily returnees, spotted him and pulled up alongside. The young man driving the truck wasted no time in issuing his instructions.

"Could you get in the back of the truck please, sir?"

"Sorry," said Charlie. "I don't think you understand. I'm on my way to Broadway Tower to meet my friends."

"If your friends were at Broadway Tower, it will have been weeks ago and they will be long gone," said the officer. "Now get in the back of the truck. I won't ask again."

To emphasise his point, another officer carrying a machine gun jumped out the back of the truck and indicated to

Charlie to climb aboard, after which he was driven to the nearby village and registered.

Despite his recent graduation from university, it was decided that he had no practical skills and he was sent to work with a road crew, who had been tasked with removing abandoned vehicles. At night, he slept in a dormitory in an old church hall. Any attempt to get news about Kaylee fell on deaf ears and he had no way of contacting her. Despite the restoration of electricity, which worked roughly half the time, it was strictly rationed, and the use of it to charge mobile phones was forbidden.

It wouldn't have helped even if he could have charged his phone, because the networks were still down. The authorities had decided that it would be best if all communication was conducted just between themselves for the time being. The last thing they wanted was people running off to find their long-lost relatives, or criticising the regime on social media. This way, it was a lot easier to keep people under control. So the phone networks stayed off indefinitely, even after the infrastructure had been restored.

Any hopes Kaylee might have had that she would find Charlie waiting for her when she eventually arrived in the future were therefore dashed. Broadway Tower was deserted when she emerged there at the end of September, leaving her no option but to descend to the village below. There, inevitably, she too was picked up by the patrols, and taken a few miles away to work in a food processing factory. Her plea that, as a meteorologist, she had a key role to play in helping farmers plan for the months ahead was ignored.

It was a similar story for the others. Josh's claim to be a mathematical genius cut no ice, so he ended up on a farm, and there was no call for Lauren's hairdressing skills and experience of working in the pub. Both were shipped off to various backbreaking tasks. Finally there was Seema, who despite being well known back in Oxfordshire for her hard-hitting journalistic skills, was virtually unknown in Worcestershire. Not that it would have done it any good. The last thing the authorities wanted was nosy journalists asking questions.

But for her and Lauren, at least, there was a happy reunion. Picked up a day apart in the same area, close to the tower, they found themselves assigned to the same work roster distributing food supplies in Evesham, where they were even eventually able to share a house. So it wasn't all doom and gloom. And after a few weeks, while Lauren was collecting food supplies from the processing plant where Kaylee worked, the two of them were also reunited.

By the middle of October, the entire population of the world had returned. Many had died, the most common reason being starvation, and they would not be the last. Restarting the world was proving to be a monumental task. It wasn't just a case of restarting the old shipping and trade lines and everyone carrying on where they had left off. Countries that had previously exported ships full of produce to the UK had no interest in doing so now. Why would they send millions of tonnes of rice, bananas, and other things that they desperately needed for themselves to the UK? They had hungry mouths of their own to feed.

The same went for oil and other fossil fuels. Countries like Russia and China had plenty, but knowing how desperate the world was, set the price ruinously high. There was talk of the UK Government allowing new drilling projects in the North Sea and building new nuclear power stations, but these things had taken years if not decades to get off the ground even in the old, properly interconnected world. It was clear that the era of rationing and power cuts was going to be a long one.

In Downing Street, with everyone returned, David had called a meeting for the most senior government members. The agenda was to thrash out a plan which they could put to the rest of the cabinet later. He had been extremely reluctant to include Jenna Rose after the way she had behaved in his absence, but she had managed to charm her way back in with more than a little help from Dominic. She claimed that if she hadn't done things the way she had done, things would have been a lot worse. Of course, there was no way to disprove this, and Simon in particular was fiercely critical of her inclusion, feeling that the energy minister should have been there instead.

And so she found herself seated around the table, along with Simon, David, and Dominic. There might just have been four of them, but the atmosphere was intense. Not only were they confronting an almost impossible situation, but the hostilities between them were greater than ever.

The two were very much split into two camps. David did not trust Dominic an inch and it was pretty obvious to whom he had pledged his allegiance. David had been thinking of getting rid of him before all this had happened, but now he was stuck with him. Dominic was extremely influential and excelled in getting things done. He had been instrumental in the restoration of the power grid, but David knew it all came at a price. He would be helpful, provided David steered policy in the way he, and more than likely Jenna as well, wanted it to go.

At least he had Simon in his camp. Good, reliable old Simon. But would his support be enough, considering how ruthless the other two could be?

Dominic had just finished summarising the latest situation regarding the power grid.

"And we're confident we can keep the lights on through the winter?" asked David.

"If we ration people to a few hours a day, yes," said Dominic.

"And what if we have a really cold winter?" said Jenna, who was eager to rock the boat. "It's a shame we didn't increase our production of North Sea oil and gas when we had the chance, isn't it? And then there was fracking. What a missed opportunity that was!"

"It's no good going on about that now," said Simon. "We inherited the previous regime's commitment to net zero when we were elected, and can hardly be blamed for not anticipating this situation."

268

"So what do you suggest we do about it?" said Jenna. You've seen the report from James Brookes. There is no prospect of us being able to start any new projects while we're in the current mess. We've got to try and make do with what we have for now."

"I still think it's worth speaking to the Russians again to see if we can negotiate a deal for some of their gas," said David,

"Fat chance of that," said Dominic. "They weren't cooperative in the best of times, what makes you think they would want to help us now? And the other countries are even worse. Have you seen how much Saudi Arabia is asking for oil? Five hundred dollars a barrel! I don't think you've going to find that down the back of the sofa."

"Sourcing energy is the least of our problems," said Jenna, keen to put the boot in. "We don't have enough food to feed everyone. And whose fault is that?"

"I hope you are not trying to imply that it's me," said David.

"If I recall correctly, you spent three years as Secretary of State for Environment, Food and Rural Affairs under the previous administration," said Jenna. "And I also recall that during that period we reduced farmland, cut down on cattle in the interests of methane reduction, and began importing a lot more food from abroad because it was cheaper. All under your watch."

"Look, Jenna," said David, feeling flustered, "We're in a tight spot here. We have a responsibility to millions of people out there and you trying to score cheap political points isn't going to help them."

"Quite right," said Simon. "I think you had more than enough to say when you had your little power-crazed episode when David was away. Now I suggest we stop arguing and start trying to find some solutions."

"Oh, I've got one," said Jenna. "But you aren't going to like it."

"Then keep it to yourself," said Simon. "I've heard enough of your vile suggestions to last a lifetime."

"I think we should listen to what Jenna has to say," said Dominic, who already knew what it was going to be. The two of them had discussed it in secret beforehand, which was when he had decided, undoubtedly that he would be better off siding with her. This had nothing to do with what was best for the country, only what was best for him. Get with the winning team, that had been the advice his grandfather had given him, and it had served him well.

"Let me put it bluntly," said Jenna. "We don't have enough energy for everyone. We lack the capacity to produce food for everyone and no one will sell us any from abroad, except at prices that would bankrupt us. Britain may have been self-sustainable hundreds of years ago but there were only a few million people here then. Quite simply, we have too many people and no way to sustain them."

"So what are you suggesting?" said David, a feeling of horror beginning to spread through him at what she might be hinting. Sure enough, her next statement confirmed it.

"That it might not do any harm if we were to lose a few people."

"You can't be serious, surely," said Simon. "You mean, as in killing them?"

"Well, not directly," said Jenna. "But a few freezing months with no heating, plus engineered food shortages, in the right areas for the right people, should naturally reduce the population to a more sustainable level."

"I can't believe I'm hearing this," said David. "I know things are hard, but if we all pull together enough, we can get through this, even if people have to survive at subsistence level for a while."

"It won't be enough, trust me. Dom, your stats people have crunched all the numbers on this already. Tell him."

"She's right," admitted Dominic. "We've modelled the figures and realistically, we can't sustain more than around thirty-five million people as things currently stand."

"But that's half the population!" exclaimed David. "Are you seriously suggesting that I instigate policies that are going to kill thirty-five million people?"

"No, to save thirty-five million and allow them to live in relative comfort a year or two from now," said Jenna "It's that

271

or have seventy million live a life of utter deprivation, struggling on the cusp of starvation for decades to come. Don't you think it would be kinder all around if half of them were put out of their misery? And, with food being so short, well, it would be a shame for their bodies to go to waste, wouldn't it?"

She delivered these lines coolly, with not a hint of concern for the people she was talking about.

"I think we should take a short break," said David, unable to conceal his disgust. "Simon, come and give me a hand with the coffee, will you?"

Staff in Downing Street were sparse. There was no calling someone to bring them coffee anymore. If they wanted some, they went to the coffee machine and fetched it themselves. This had been David's idea. He did not see why they should be waited on while everyone else was wearing their fingers to their bones.

For now, David wasn't bothered about the coffee. He just wanted to get out of the room and speak to Simon away from the other two. It was obvious what he was doing and he knew Jenna and Dominic would see through it, but it didn't matter. He could not stay in the room and debate what she was proposing any longer.

They went and got coffee anyway, and at the machine he discussed his concerns with Simon, who he knew would feel exactly like he did.

"Can you honestly believe what she just said?"

"I'm afraid I can," said Simon. "She made life in the bunker a living hell when we were stuck down there for weeks. I don't believe there is anything she's not capable of."

"It's inhuman," said David. "No, that's not strong enough. It's evil. We can't allow this."

"I told you not to bring her back into the fold. She's dangerous. We need to replace her as soon as possible. And you can get rid of Dom while you're at it."

But it was potentially already too late. Up in the conference room, Jenna and Dominic were reaching similar conclusions about David and Simon.

"Come on, Dom, you can see how weak David is. He doesn't have what it takes to handle a situation like this. The people need strong leadership and that means making tough decisions. Are you with me, or against me?"

Dom thought it over but there was never really any doubt what he was going to do. David hadn't said anything in the meeting to encourage him to think that there was any future supporting him. The plan Jenna had put forward was barbaric but he had to think about his own prospects. Decades of poverty for the nation didn't sound much fun, even if doubtless it would provide opportunities to feather his own nest.

"You know that David and Simon will never agree to this, don't you?" he said.

"You're right, they won't, and that means they'll drag us down with them. So, the way I see it, that only leaves us with one option."

"You don't mean what I think you mean, do you?"

"Yes, I do. And I know you're the man to get it done. You know people. And it's not like you haven't done it before."

"Maybe I have, but nothing like on this scale. You're talking about murdering the Prime Minister."

"Desperate times call for desperate measures. We live in dangerous times. Anything could happen. Providing it looks like an accident, there's nothing to trace it back to us. Oh, and if Simon were to meet a similar fate, I wouldn't shed any tears. That man's been a thorn in my side too long."

Dominic sat back and weighed up his options. What she was proposing was beyond the pale. When he had allied himself with her, it had been more to depose David, not dispose of him completely. Besides, despite their differences he liked David. He wasn't exactly a friend – people like Dominic didn't have friends – but he was agreeable company, especially outside work. He couldn't do it.

Could he?

Chapter Twenty
May 2027

Nearly four years later, Seema Mistry, the newly elected Prime Minister of the United Kingdom, stood at a lectern outside the front door of 10 Downing Street on a pleasant Friday morning. She could scarcely believe the speech she was about to give.

She was not the youngest Prime Minister in British history. That accolade belonged to William Pitt the Younger, but even so, at thirty-one, despite all she had been through, she felt as if she were way too inexperienced to be in this position. But it was a position she had earned, having swept the board at the election on a tide of votes from a grateful nation.

It was an electorate that had every reason to show her gratitude. The years since the mysterious event, still referred to as the Rapture, had been tough beyond belief, and it had been she more than anyone else who had led the country out of the darkness.

She hadn't intended to be a freedom fighter. All she had when she and Lauren found themselves sent to a work camp in Wales, was an unbreakable spirit, and a determination to find out the truth about what was going on there.

Allegedly there to assist in the rebuilding effort, it quickly became clear to the two of them that there was something sinister going on. There was very little to do on the disused army base on which they had been effectively interned, with virtually nothing to eat. Within a few days, they realised the awful truth. They and everyone else in the camp had been sent there to die. Some had succumbed already.

If it had not been for Lauren, she doubted she would have made it through. Together, before they grew too weak from hunger, they began to plan an escape and organise a resistance. It was a tough ask, as many in the camp believed the relentless propaganda that this was all just down to the food shortages and that they had to just wait a while longer and then things would get better. They simply could not accept that the authorities would deliberately kill their own people. Their faith was unfounded, and most of them died.

Seema, Lauren, and a few brave others managed to break out of the base and go underground, where they spent several months camping out in a disused railway tunnel. During that first winter they were on the brink of starvation, but just about managed to survive by foraging, hunting and stealing.

All the while, Jenna and Dominic continued to roll out their evil plan across the country. There was no one in the way to stop them. David and Simon were dead, their car hit head on with a truck whilst being escorted to an emergency energy meeting just outside London. Far from distancing himself from the crime, Dominic actively hinted to everyone he dealt with that anyone who did not toe the line might find themselves suffering a similar fate. Thus, they were able to watch from afar as their plan to depopulate the country came to fruition. He even made sure he was supplied with a daily running total of the deaths with which he was able to brief Jenna with each morning, something she seemed to almost take pleasure in.

Seema and Lauren were not the only ones who had figured out the truth. Across the country, other resistance groups formed and it wasn't just those in the camps that were pushing back. Many of those who had been deemed useful by the regime and allowed to live lives of relative comfort had worked it out and began to form networks of people determined to fight back. Belonging to such groups was fraught with danger, and many were caught and executed under the emergency powers.

They were the brave ones. There were many more, particularly during that first year, who knew deep down what was going on but chose to ignore it. It was easier to go along with the narrative and save themselves than to admit the truth.

Eventually, like most tyrants, Jenna got too greedy. Figuring out that the fewer useless eaters there were in the country, the greater her level of luxury would become, she began to order more and more people to the camps, including many who had worked hard with great loyalty over the previous couple of years. By now, Seema was establishing herself as the head of the resistance and her voice could be heard across the nation every day, as she made regular broadcasts on short-wave radio to a nation that was rapidly waking up to what was being done to them.

She and Lauren barely stayed one night in the same place, as they were always on the move to avoid capture. They spent their time meeting up with other groups and were delighted one evening in Bristol to be reunited with Josh, Charlie, and

Kaylee. They had found each other again when sent to a similar disused base to the one in which Seema and Lauren had been incarcerated, and had been the driving force behind forming their local resistance group.

Seema's broadcasts had come to Jenna's attention, and she had ordered that both she and Lauren, who occasionally added her own contributions, no longer be captured. She wanted them shot on sight, but somehow they always managed to stay one step ahead of their pursuers. As time passed, it got easier, as many of those with orders to track them down agreed with what they were doing.

The turning point came just before Christmas 2026 when an army patrol caught Seema and Lauren red-handed. They thought they were going to be executed on the spot but instead, the captain in charge welcomed them with open arms and hailed them as heroes. The army was no longer willing to carry out Jenna's orders and was preparing for revolution. They saw Seema and Lauren as the leaders to inspire the people to rise up.

They were right. In what became known as the Valentine's Revolution in February 2027, the nation rose up behind Seema, stormed parliament, and took Jenna, Dominic, and several other crooked members of their regime prisoner. With the mood of the crowd, they were lucky not to have been killed on the spot, but Seema had insisted they were taken alive so they could stand trial for their crimes.

In addition, she refused to accept the mantle of leader which many were keen to thrust upon her immediately. She insisted, that after over three years of tyranny, the due democratic process was followed and proper elections held. In the meantime, she agreed to take the position of acting leader, making it clear that it was only temporary until the outcome of the elections was known.

At first, she had not intended to stand for the role of leader, not seeing herself as a natural politician. It wasn't a profession she had ever had any sort of respect for, having spent much of her early journalistic career giving them a hard time. But it was impossible to ignore the overwhelming support the nation had for her. That applied to Lauren too, and she was persuaded to stand for a neighbouring seat.

The election result was a foregone conclusion, with the newly formed Freedom Party winning over 90% of the seats, an unprecedented result. The old parties were virtually wiped out, most notably the party of Jenna Rose, which did not win a single seat. Now Seema, with the voice that had been a comfort to so many on the radio during the past couple of years, stood at the lectern and began to speak.

"Today, we welcome a new dawn for our great nation, a dawn of hope and freedom where we leave the tyranny and suffering of the past few years behind us. Few among us have not suffered. Those that came before me brought misery, starvation, and death, through their policies which were at best misguided, and at worst, evil. But now, they have been vanquished, yet I stand before you as the new Prime Minister, not as a conqueror, but as a servant of the people, ready to lead us all into a brighter future.

"I am honoured by the trust you have placed in me and our new democratically elected government. The road that brought us here was long and arduous, with countless sacrifices, and millions of lives lost. Our hearts mourn for the loved ones we lost along the way, and their memory will guide us to ensure that whatever challenges our nation may face in the future, we will never wilfully inflict such suffering again.

"I know many among you believe that no mercy should be shown to the leaders of the previous regime, and I am aware of the penalties that many of you believe they should suffer. I do not wish to comment on that at this juncture, all I will say is that it is essential that they be tried in accordance with our laws, and they will be held in custody until due process can be carried out. The only comment I am willing to make is that the end can never justify the means."

"That bitch Rose wants stringing up!" exclaimed Andy, who was watching, back on his favourite bar stool, in the recently reopened Red Lion.

The worst of the food and drink shortages were over, after three harvests, and the opening up once again of affordable trade with the rest of the world. That meant that the pub was once again a viable business, and none was happier than Andy.

There was a murmuring of agreement around him at the bar, concerning his comment about the hated Jenna Rose, as the assorted regulars watched the speech on the pub's television.

"She should be tried as a war criminal, certainly," said Kent, also back in his familiar place behind the bar.

"Look, there's Lauren!" said Nobby, spotting their former barmaid standing alongside Seema. "I voted for her!"

"And now she's our MP," said Kent. "Which rules her out of coming back to work here. Pity."

"Bit of a claim to fame, though, eh?" said Andy. "For all of us. I nearly shagged her once, you know."

"No, you didn't, Andy," said Kent. "Stop bullshitting."

"Whatever. As long as she sorts out the beer supply, she'll keep my vote. I can't believe you ran out last week."

"Well, if you didn't drink so much of it, perhaps it would last longer."

"I don't see you complaining," said Andy.

"I'm not, but your girlfriend will be if you start spending all your time in here again."

"I still can't believe he's got a girlfriend," said Nobby.

"Yes, he met her when we were on the farm. For some reason none of us can fathom, she seemed to think he was a nice bloke."

"Has she got a white stick?" asked Nobby.

"No, it defies all logic. Still, she's bound to rumble him eventually," said Kent. "Then he'll be back to crying into his beer in here, morning, noon and night."

"You don't know anything about it," said Andy, who wasn't much one for talking about his feelings, but things between him and Maria had blossomed in the time they had spent together on the farm and he was optimistic about their chances of a future together.

The thing he wasn't happy about was the frequent beer shortages, especially now he no longer had access to the farm's supply of cider. Despite the return to semi-normality, it seemed like supply problems were going to be a feature of life for some years to come. At least things had reached the point of inconvenience now, rather than a risk to life. After what the country had been through, few people complained about the two or three power cuts a week, or if they couldn't get any bananas for weeks at a time. Things were haphazard, but there was always something to eat, even if it wasn't one's first choice.

Back on TV, a form of entertainment that had recently returned after over three years off the air, Seema was reaching the climax of her speech.

"As we step into this new era, we must learn from the lessons of the past. The scars of suffering and loss will serve as a constant reminder of the importance of upholding the values that define us as a nation. We must never forget the price so many paid to restore our freedom, for it is through remembering them that we create a better future for all.

"In the years to come, we will face challenges but we shall overcome them together. We will continue to rebuild our communities, our infrastructure, and our relationships and I would urge you all to mend broken bridges and leave past differences behind. Then, together, as a united nation, we shall prosper once again.

"Thank you for electing me, and I give you my commitment that I will serve you with honesty, integrity and a steadfast commitment to the principles that brought us here today. Together, let us write a new chapter in the story of our beloved United Kingdom, a chapter filled with compassion, progress, and hope. Thank you."

She stepped back from the podium to rapturous applause, not just from those present in Downing Street, but across the nation where crowds had been celebrating all night in town squares in a way the country had not seen since VE Day.

They were all still none the wiser as to the cause of the strange phenomenon that had transported them forward in time. It seemed it was a mystery that would forever remain unsolved, but for now, all that mattered was that they were free.

Chapter Twenty-one
August 2059

"So, did we do the right thing?" asked Alice.

The crowds across Britain in May 2027 were not the only people watching Seema's landmark speech.

Over thirty years in the future, in a different universe, a group of time travellers had been reviewing everything that had happened, from the motorway crash that had started it all right up to Seema's speech.

"I believe so," said Josh, as they watched Seema on the big screen in his lab in Oxford. This was a different version of Josh, now in his fifties, whose counterpart in the other reality had been part of the group that had fled the chaos in search of sanctuary at Broadway Tower.

With him was his wife Alice, and Henry Jones, a scientist from Australia who had settled in the UK and now worked with Josh at the lab. Watching on, was Henry's faithful robot companion, Dani. He had not met any of them at the time of the events that had been watching, though both Alice and Henry had taken a peek at their own counterpart's experience. Both had been through similar traumatic journeys but had survived.

"What's this?" asked Lauren, who had just pushed open the doors to the lab and come in, glancing at the screen to see what they were watching. "Hey, that's Seema, when she was young. What's she doing outside Downing Street?"

"We're watching a stream from another universe," said Josh. "One you visited when you went on your little odyssey a couple of months ago."

"Hardly little," said Lauren, looking at the screen. "So which universe is this? I don't recognise it."

"You wouldn't. It's the Gamma universe. You visited it in 1984. We're watching a feed from 2027."

"Hey, that's me!" said Lauren, spotting herself next to Seema. "What am I doing there? And why am I so thin? I never had a figure that good."

"Yes, well, there wasn't a lot of food around at the time," said Josh. "You won't see any overweight people on this feed."

"So what's going on there?" asked Lauren. "Why are Seema and I in Downing Street and why are we so well dressed? Look at me! I'm in a business suit! I've never worn a business suit in my life. It makes me look important. Am I?"

"Perhaps we had better fill you in on the story," suggested Alice.

"Yes, please do!" said Lauren. "But can we do it over a drink? Stories always go down better with a drop of vodka, I find."

"I'd be up for that," said Henry. "Dani can keep an eye on things here, can't you, Dani?"

"Affirmative," said the android without a hint of jealousy. There was a bit of a potential love triangle going on with Lauren dropping plenty of hints that she was interested in Henry lately, despite him being in a physical relationship with the android. Thankfully, Dani didn't have emotions, which was perhaps just as well. Lauren had endured enough grief from Alice over the years who remained resentful of their relationship from forty years ago, and the last thing she needed was a jealous robot too.

The four of them made their way to their favourite haunt, The Turf Tavern, where they took their drinks to the walled garden at the rear and Josh told the tale of their latest project.

"After you returned from your trip, Dani spent some more time analysing the history of the various universes you visited and discovered something rather disturbing, didn't she, Henry?"

"She did," replied Henry. "The gamma universe had proceeded forward from the year you left it, more or less in parallel with ours. There were a few differences – notably on the political front, where the change to a proportional voting system led to a completely different set of politicians running the country by the 2020s to the ones we remember."

"And that's how Seema and I ended up in Downing Street?" asked Lauren. "Wow!"

"Not exactly," said Josh. "There's a lot more to it than that. You see, what you are seeing on the screen now never happened in the universe's original timeline."

"What do you mean, original timeline?" asked Lauren. "Are you telling me it's changed?"

"I am," said Josh. "And we are the ones that changed it."

"And why would you want to do that?"

"Oh, we had a very good reason," said Josh. "Though Alice still isn't convinced."

"Did you hear what Seema said in her speech about the end never justifying the means?" replied Alice. "Rather thought-provoking, don't you think?"

"But under the circumstances…" began Henry.

"What circumstances?" asked Lauren, intrigued. "Just tell me what you did."

"OK, well, it's like this," said Josh. "When Dani looked into the future of the universe after you left it, she discovered something shocking. Everything was fine, up until the summer of 2023. Then, almost overnight, everybody died."

"How?" asked Lauren.

"That's what we had to find out," said Josh. "And it wasn't just the people. One day, all animal life, from elephants to the smallest-sized amoeba, simply perished. We were looking

287

at a dead planet, at least in terms of animal life. Though, strangely, the vegetation was unaffected."

"Obviously, we couldn't risk going there to find out why, in case whatever killed them, killed us," added Henry. "So we sent Dani, figuring that being an artificial life form, she would be safe. Which she was."

"What did she find out?" asked Lauren.

"She examined some of the bodies and discovered that every single cell in their bodies had been destroyed by a lethal dose of radiation."

"From where?" asked Lauren. "Was there a nuclear war or something?"

"No, nothing like that," said Josh. "Dani went back to the day they all died to try and find out why, where she witnessed an incredible event. We watched the recording she sent back, which showed the world being enveloped by an incredible pink light, which spread across the skies, creating a spectacular but deadly light show. At first, people marvelled at the display but their delight was short-lived. The light was a cloud of lethal radioactive dust, which subjected all animal material to an unimaginable assault. The lethal radiation permeated through their bodies, disrupting the delicate balance of cellular structures. It infiltrated their DNA strands, causing horrific mutations and damage at an unprecedented rate."

"It killed them all?" asked Lauren.

"And very quickly," replied Josh. "They died in agony, within minutes, every cell in their bodies utterly destroyed."

"But what caused it?"

"That's what we needed to find out, so Dani, working with Alice, who is as you know an astrophysicist, went back in time to before the event and observed a comet approaching the planet. One that thankfully does not exist in our universe or any other."

"How can that be?" asked Lauren. "I thought cosmic events were fixed, and it was only when we went back in time and did things that we could alter things down here on Earth."

"Not in this case, it seems," said Alice. "Anyway, this comet was unlike any other encountered before, but scientists on Earth didn't seem particularly worried about it. It wasn't even that big. There was some talk of potential meteor showers but that was about it. They had no idea of the malevolent payload it was about to unleash on the planet. I attempted to warn them, but no one was interested."

"And even if they had listened, what could they have done?" said Henry. "Everyone was doomed. They had no way of detecting the true nature of the comet, which was composed of a deadly radioactive element, hitherto unknown to humanity. It was a dark anomaly that seemed to defy the laws of known physics because the existence of this element was not even theoretically possible, according to the laws of the periodic table. All we knew was that it was lethal."

"But it didn't destroy plant life?" asked Lauren.

"No," said Henry, "which led us to speculate that it might have been some sort of weapon, designed to strip a planet of its existing animal life, but leaving a thriving supply of vegetation. Perhaps ahead of an alien colonisation. But we looked into the future, and no aliens ever arrived. As for the comet, it did not appear to be being steered by anyone and continued through the cosmos on a predictable path, rounding the sun and heading back to beyond the outer reaches of the solar system."

"The interesting thing about this radioactive element was that it decayed very quickly," added Alice. "Within a couple of days, all trace of it was gone, and the planet was perfectly habitable again."

"Where the comet came from or why were questions we couldn't answer," said Josh. "But we then began to ask ourselves, could we do anything about it?"

"And presumably you could?" said Lauren. "Judging by the pictures on the screen you were watching when I came in."

"Yes," said Josh. "I had been working for some time on a device that could generate time bubbles at random, and we figured out that we could adapt it to attempt something on a scale far grander than anything we had ever done before."

"We decided that we were going to evacuate the entire population of Earth," said Alice.

"Evacuate where?" asked Lauren.

"Not where," said Josh. "But, when. We adapted my experiment to create time bubbles all over the planet, in all manner of shapes and sizes. They were designed to pick up any living being of animal origin they could find. When they encountered an organism, they threw it forward in time by several weeks to a point after the comet had passed through."

"But that must have been an enormous task!" exclaimed Lauren. "I mean how many of these bubbles did you need?"

"Trillions," said Josh. "And there was a limit to how many we could generate at a time. Think of those bubble-blowing toys that kids play with. We were constantly blowing out bubbles, all over the planet, for over a month."

"And did you do it?"

"Yes," said Josh. "The bubbles were trained to detect animal life, almost like heat-seeking missiles. When there were only a few people left, they hunted them down, until all were gone. When the comet came, filling the skies with its lethal light show, there was nobody left on the planet to see it."

"So you saved everyone?" asked Lauren. "That's amazing!"

"Not exactly, no," said Alice. "The population of Earth was about eight billion when all this started. Three years later, it was down to six billion."

"So, a quarter of the world's population died?" asked Lauren. "How?"

"You can't just leave the planet empty of people for a few weeks and then expect it to just start up again," said Alice. "Our whole world runs like clockwork on set things happening at set times. Stop that, and the consequences are catastrophic. And as for the six billion that did survive, life was no picnic for them for a long time afterwards. The effects are being felt even now. In their version of 2059, people are a lot less prosperous than they are here."

"I have to admit, the outcome was a lot worse than we thought it was going to be," said Josh. "Which is why we've been debating whether we should have done it or not."

"Of course, you should have done it!" said Lauren. "You saved six billion people!"

"And killed two billion," replied Alice.

"Who would have died anyway," said Lauren.

"Well, therein lies part of the debate," said Alice. "You see, we started taking people several weeks before the comet came. Some of those people came to horrific ends when they emerged from their time bubbles. For example, those who had been on aeroplanes at the time found themselves thirty thousand feet up in the air with no parachute."

"Yes, but they would still have died when the comet came," said Lauren.

"But not until several weeks later," said Alice. "Do you see my point? We stole those weeks from their lives. In effect, we murdered them."

"Gosh, when you put it that way, you have a point," said Lauren. "This is like one of those moral dilemmas where there is not one right or wrong answer."

"In her speech we just watched, Seema talked about the end never justifying the means," said Alice. "She was talking about the actions of a ruthless dictator who tried to starve half the population to death so that she and others could have comfortable lives. Is what we did that much different?"

"In this case?" said Henry. "I'm sorry, but I agree with Josh. I still think we did the right thing."

"I'm inclined to agree with you," said Lauren. "Six billion people are alive and well who weren't before you intervened. Plus goodness knows how many other animals and insects. Anyway, putting that aside for a moment, I'm intrigued to find out why Seema is outside the Prime Minister's house giving a speech."

"Because in the altered timeline, she has become Prime Minister," said Henry.

"Wow, really? How?"

"Well, things were incredibly bleak after people arrived in the future after their trip through time. The world was in a mess, and some bad people seized control of the country. They murdered the Prime Minister and Chancellor of the Exchequer, making it look like an accident, of course," said Henry.

"The new leader, Jenna Rose, was the ruthless dictator I mentioned earlier," said Alice. "She instigated policies that were

293

tantamount to murdering her own people. There were even suggestions of using the dead bodies for food to alleviate the food shortages."

"You mean cannibalism?" asked a horrified Lauren.

"Yes," replied Alice, "though we can't find any evidence that did happen in the end. Perhaps it was a step too far for the military and Jenna backed down. But she would have done it if she could have got away with it, from what we've seen of her. And you would have been one of those being eaten. Both you and Seema were on the death list and were sent to what was the equivalent of a prisoner of war camp, where together the two of you formed a resistance."

"Seema and I, eh?" said Lauren. "That's interesting, bearing in mind what happened when I met her before. Can I assume we got together in more ways than one?"

"You did," said Josh. "To cut a long story short, it took a few years but eventually you overthrew the government and restored democracy. Both of you were elected, her as Prime Minister, and she gave you the post of Home Secretary."

"That's incredible," said Lauren. "I mean, not just us getting elected but that she and I got together and started a revolution. Because it's not the first time something like this has happened. When I went to the beta universe, I met another Seema who was fighting back against the oppressive social credit system they had there. We got together then, too."

"It is interesting how these patterns replicate themselves across different timelines, I must concur," said Josh.

"It's why I've come here today, actually," said Lauren. "To ask you if you can send me on another journey. When I was in that other universe, Seema told me that an older version of me came back to tell her when and where to meet her, when I first encountered her in Hyde Park. Well, I haven't done that yet, so presumably at some point, I'll need to go back and do it. That is how all this time travel stuff works, isn't it?"

"Indeed it is," said Josh. "We can do it when we get back from the pub if you like?"

"There's no hurry," said Lauren. "I could do with a couple more vodkas first, you know, to relax me a bit for the journey."

"Isn't this just more tinkering?" asked Alice.

"What Lauren is describing has technically already happened," said Josh. "We have no choice. She has to go."

"Of course she does," said Alice. "And what is the next project to be? You've been promising to give this up now ever since the first lot of trouble we had with Vanessa, four years ago. But something else always comes up, doesn't it? There's always one more adventure."

"Oh, yes, there will definitely be one more adventure," said Josh. "I don't know what it is going to be, yet. But I'm sure I'll think of something."

"I'm sure you will," said Alice.

THE END…for now.

Reviews

Before you go, may I ask a small favour?

As an independent author, I don't have the strength of a big marketing budget behind me. I rely on word of mouth to spread the word about my books, plus genuine reviews from enthusiastic readers who have enjoyed the book. These encourage potential new readers to try a story from an author they haven't read before.

If you enjoyed these books, I would be hugely grateful if you would consider taking a few minutes to leave a short review on the Amazon website. It all helps with getting the books in front of new readers, even if it is only a couple of short sentences.

The Time Bubble Collection

If you missed any of the earlier books in the series, please head over to my author page on Amazon where you can find them individually, or in box sets:

1) The Time Bubble
2) Global Cooling
3) Man Out of Time
4) Splinters in Time
5) Class of '92
6) Vanishing Point
7) Midlife Crisis
8) Rock Bottom
9) My Tomorrow, Your Yesterday
10) Happy New Year
11) Return to Tomorrow
12) Cause of Death
13) Lauren's Odyssey
14) Gone to the Rapture

UK Link:

https://www.amazon.co.uk/Jason-Ayres/e/B00CQO4XJC/

US Link:

https://www.amazon.com/Jason-Ayres/e/B00CQO4XJC/

The Ronnie and Bernard Adventures

The Ronnie and Bernard Adventures are a set of humorous novels, with mild science fiction and horror elements, set in the 1970s. The stories follow the fortunes of two actors from very different backgrounds.

Together, they tackle mysteries, travel in time, and negotiate the rocky path of life as jobbing actors, from daytime soaps to panto.

Anyone who remembers the 1970s will love these nostalgic stories looking back at a time when life was simpler, and the world didn't take itself too seriously. Packed with period detail, humour, and references to the era, they are the perfect antidote to modern living.

1) The Crooked Line
2) The Haunted Theatre

UK Link:

https://www.amazon.co.uk/Jason-Ayres/e/B0BR9SMPPY/

US Link:

https://www.amazon.com/Jason-Ayres/e/B0BR9SMPPY/

About the Author

Jason Ayres lives in the market town of Evesham with his wife and two sons.

Following a lengthy career in market research, he turned his hand to writing, releasing the first Time Bubble book in the summer of 2014. Over a dozen books later, the series is still going strong.

Want to know more about Jason?

You can find his official website here:

https://www.jasonayres.co.uk/

Find him on Twitter:

https://twitter.com/TheTimeBubble/

Or check out his Facebook page for the latest news:

https://www.facebook.com/TheTimeBubble/

And for lots more Time Bubble related stuff, including a podcast, subscribe to the YouTube channel:

https://www.youtube.com/channel/UCg13jmfTUTFCqWWZrPmXqJQ